CW00428286

Rapture World VI

Predeterminism

Predeterminism Series book 4 of 6

1st Science Prediction Fiction story written

By

C.A FENDERSON JR.

This novel is a fictional post-apocalyptic portrayal of the world destroyed and rekindled by the new laws of the Gods. Philosophy, theory, and science.

Copyright © 2016 by C.A Fenderson Jr.

All rights reserved. No part of this publication may be reproduced, distributed, or transmitted in any form or by any means, including photocopying, recording, or other electronic or mechanical methods, without the prior written permission of the publisher, except in the case of brief quotations embodied in critical reviews and certain other noncommercial uses permitted by copyright law.

ISBN-13: 9781537397559

ISBN-10: 1537397559

This is a work of fiction. Names, characters, businesses, places, events, and incidents either are the products of the author's imagination or used in a fictitious manner. Any resemblance to actual persons, living or dead, or actual events is purely coincidental.

DEDICATION

To my kids. You have kept me determined through this dream the whole time. Thank you for keeping me active and thinking of you. Love always. Dad. I would also like to dedicate this series to my father. May you rest is paradise.

Prologue

Chapters

Rapture World, New World

1

2

3

Underground World

4

5

6

7

8

9

10

11

Latady, Antarctica Island

12

THERE IS NO JOY IN THE SUNTIMES. Heaven could not exist viewing the sun once a week throughout your captivity, confined within a realm which criminals are bound and pardoned unbearably. These reformers seek to gather in friendships within *sun-times*, which take place once a week in the 6th Realm- highest of all realms in the Rapture world. A domain harvesting criminals before you reach the death realm of Rapture *Zell*. These reformers would be amongst few who will reach Raptures 5 and 6. To even partake in a friendship during the *sun-times,* gives reformers a chance to listen to tales of previous Rotters (prisoner in a rapture realm), and the progression to make it to the highest Rapture before returning into society. The 2nd and 3rd Raptures are horrid. You must pray and hope the Angels of the Angelic Realm only deposits souls and not dispose of yours into the dimension known as Rapture *Zell*. In the sixth Rapture, seeing the *sun-times* and possibly joining a friendship, an hour a week is not near hell or in this case near Rapture *Zell*.

Most mind-*stalks* have made it into the rapture worlds for manipulating others to commit crimes, including the ultimately governed law crime, death. Even though every living soul in the new world has a knowledge of the Angelic Realm, and surrenders the importance of every person to keep the world alive as a *faith citizen* -still *mind stalks,* and others remain criminal. The new world is full of criminals, artists of deceit, The Global Council, and countless other sects. To keep the present shift of the new world, every soul must do its part to produce submerging energy of faith to the God Realm.

Unfortunately, *mind stalks* and others purposefully destroy those citizen's efforts, jeopardizing the new world for their personal gaining pleasures, *defying truth*. There are many new laws in the new world which every citizen must obey. If people do not follow these rules, they are subject to the

Angelic Realm for judgment, by either cast into the lower realms or by death. The demons who cast do not feel and are spirits from heaven doing the work of the Gods. When a citizen breaks the law of killing a person in the new world, including taken their life, supernatural beings appear from the sky, to do the Gods deeds of punishment. The citizens of the new world have locked themselves inside of their homes to avoid manipulation, and what The Global Council has termed –*Predeterminism*, and to abide by The Great Truth Announcement.

THE WORLD has been devastated over the last decades. Countless wars. Could you imagine living through the end of the world? At least I was a quiet yet tempered schooled church boy in Cuenca, Ecuador. *Thinking about it now, I been preparing for it. The rekindled last days.* The only Mom I knew was Sister Romas, my foster Mom. I loved her more than anything I did. I am never going to give up searching for her.

I have no respect for my biological Mother, a damned alcoholic she was. Tried searching for her after I ran away from the church when I was young. I never knew my Father's name, nor do I care. A dumped offed child from the beginning you can say, never knowing his real parents. Left me traumatized, although somehow- I guess you can say supernaturally, not the causes of the anxieties I suffer with now, unfortunately.

I am of flesh and blood. Homo sapiens sapiens. When cut, I will wear my mistakes, and while these wounds are healing, I learn. I have to control these thoughts in my head, not to go crazy. I pretend to be intelligent- stronger than I appear. Over here, working out and trying to keep your physique is challenging. It is wise using regularity to your advantage to maintain sanity. An average thirty-three-year-old depressed hermit, desperate and lost. Banished to another realm or dimension, outside the world we live in. Only a few more days here until I return to the new world, I hope.

I grab some tree bark making a cup shape to store rainwater; then I start a fire to boil the impurities clean. Let the water sit for an hour, giving it relentless positivity- obviously not having the resources to implode water efficiently. I could never consume without doing this. The precipitating liquid is poisonous due to the toxic atmosphere and radiation in the sky.

The time that we know of back on earth does not exist. Not here. We are captives in an imprisoned realm. Trapped. Winds scream above us; we cover our ears. Few of us speak of this terror. I converse a rodent, selfish with our food. Literally scavenging for meals with a rat who knows his way around this so-called dimensional world, more than I do. What's could be worst?

Lost in another realm- a rodent knows more than me. Crazy. Huh.

I find a rock and scrap '*Day 28* on a boulder. I found this cave the day I reported here and made it my home. I make fires on cold nights, keeping away predators, so I stay warm. Nigel, I named the rat, bites at this dead Rotter- who descended a week ago. *What do I care if a measly rat eats from a corpse?* Well, what killed this person unnaturally could cause the rat to die by eating his remains. Unless the man was scared to death, perhaps. *Damn!*

"So, let's see if I can get this scenario straight? The mysterious Rotter apparently witnessed the destruction of the world back on Earth- perversely living through the aftermath, cast to the realm we are in by a demoniacal Angel or evil spirit. Whatever you want to call it. Then, he finally has the nerve to croak when he got here, of all other events preexisting?"

Wow. A disgusting ass corpse, a scavenger rat, and I- myself talking to one. *This is so damn sad.* Not the situation I am in, no that is actually pleasant. *Ha.* No, it is sad that everyone talks to himself or herself, but at the same time are critical of people thinking aloud. *I am not going to lose my mind stuck here. I have to stay on schedule.*

I hate running behind, as I get ready for the friendships in the *sun-times*. Went most of the night in pain, digging bacteria out of my left ear. Could not go back to sleep. Nigel cannot eat all the insects we have infesting the cave. Wait until I explain what I went through last night. I stumble up a steep hill following a mob of Rotters heading towards the sun. No one sees me coming or going from this place. If they do come down, some traps I made will turn them back. I work to loosen a shiny rock I notice going up the hill. My nerves tremble picking up this rock during these sun-times for some reason. I pretend the rock has unique powers, leaving its light blueish hue behind, and turn up the blind side of the hill to run towards the group.

"Thomas. That is your name right?" I joke to a friend I catch up with. "You are Thomas of Rapture 6th?" No one can remember personal details, like their name, for example, first few days coming to the rapture.

"Duke of Dumb. I must be." He moans.

"Don't even ask!" I take my palm and cover my ear in discomfort. *How embarrassing.* Thomas is one of the people I made my friend when he first reported here. It is day 10 for him, and this will be his second *sun-times* in the 6th Rapture. The trail to the viewing point for the sun-times is quite a distance away. Talking with Thomas makes the dangerous journey bearable. I witnessed a Rotter die trying to make this trip the previous week. It is always best to have a wingman who you depend on. I hope I am Thomas's wingman. *It is important to have someone feel like I understand him or her.* People need to know that you are willing to listen to them.

The Guides supply us with enough information to stay alive if you manage to pay them for their services. Still, cannot figure what someone would possibly want for payment here, except to get the hell out. Today, the well-known Guide named Arroyo is leading the sun-times. Our sun-times

Guide challenges our pace through dense fog and mud dunes. The Guides walking cane splits beating a Rotter's back, whom we have to rescue from falling in a craven. This helpless Rotter has lost us 15 minutes of the sun-times, and no one is pleased.

Suddenly clouds separate in the sky. The doing of the Angels. The spirits can change the aspects of this realm, many people believe. No one knows for sure if this is true, but we all know that the God Realm can recreate the new world. I make a quick pass by Thomas to reach our guide, Arroyo. Not a good idea, but I want to see if I can get some answers from him.

"Hey, I see some of the clouds are starting to separate. Do you know if the Angels can rekindle?" I feel reluctant to ask. Not surprised that Arroyo does not give me an answer. His left brow starts to pull as he sweats more, surprised to hear me speak. It is almost as if he curses me to say a word to him. As I return down where I had left Thomas, another Rotter overhears my question to Arroyo. The Rotter is the same person that fell into the craven. I almost entirely ignore the sap, as I pass him by; placed in the center behind the leaders not to slow us down.

"You should not speak of the ones who appear out of the sky. The spirits who cast or the Gods who can rekindle the earth." He utters, as another Rotter hits him with a walking stick to shut him up.

What does that mean?

As I finally reach Thomas, I notice that the pace of the group speeds up double time. This is strange because we still have a long walk ahead of us, and we should be conserving energy. I do not want to question Arroyo again today, although something tells me inadvertently- I changed the pace.

Change or an anomaly does not happen in the new world. Everything that happens on the planet back home is on purpose. Yet here in the Rapture, incongruity is, unfortunately, typical. I have never seen an Angel cast someone here during the sun-times, this does not usually happen. *What if the Rotter who fell into the Craven, is actually right?* I should not have brought up the Angels.

Our group stumbles off rough terrain through cracks and ditches, moving faster. *I wonder what is going on.* Birds in the sky are just like hungry bats who react and prey on high body temperatures. If you fall to the ground, you could get bacteria infested insects between your clothing, giving off instant infection. I sneeze as the wind separates the dirt from around us. I quickly replenish my thirst with the last of my water.

"What is happening?" Thomas yells to me. "This didn't happen last time. Why are we moving so fast Duke?" He turns to confront me, frantic.

He gets his foot jammed under a covered log. Crashing down on his bone, he starts cursing in agony.

I take a desperate leap over Thomas to keep up on my feet and notice two inches of his femur protruding, as he snatches his leg from under the log. "Oh my God, Thomas!" I shout out, racing back towards him. "Arroyo, please wait!" Blood begins to stream out all over. I turn back to see Thomas on the ground grasping his injury, squirming in my direction. I look up towards our passageway to witness the last Rotter disappear in the distance through the fog. My heart races in panic as I strain someone else's voice over to the far left. *This can't be happening right now!*

2

THE CLOUDS begin to whirlwind in the sky with darkness. Insects consume the trail of pooling blood from Thomas's leg as the high winds scatter away from the birds. I start attending to Thomas, and we hear an unfamiliar sound echo in the distance heading closer to us.

"Wait for me. Please, hold on. The other Rotters attacked me." He cries thick barely finishes his sentence, passing out in front of us. The Rotter had fallen earlier, running towards us with a deep wound on the top of his head. He is losing more blood than Thomas is, and somehow he is still alive. *Why would they attack him and why did the others leave us?* I wonder to myself and quickly begin administering first aid to Thomas. I reached into my bag, grabbing a cloth to wrap up his severely damaged leg, and then I spot Nigel dash pass me out of one of the pockets. He darts through the puddles of blood away from us. Not more than ten yards away, Nigel runs through a colonel of giant ants, which immediately chew him into pieces.

"Nigel! Nigel, no!" I scream in disbelief. "That's it; let's get the hell out of here, right now!" I slow Thomas's bleeding with some applied pressure and make a brace from the walking sticks, the best I can. *There is no way the other Rotter is going to make it.* Gather what we desperately need from both of their bags. With one knee bent, push of a tree I dip Thomas across my shoulder and then stumble us off the distance.

We make it two hundred yards and start to hear creatures attack and feast on the body of the Rotter we had to leave behind to die. Manage to carry Thomas across my back, almost more two miles from where we were totaling three hours until I am completed exhausted. *I can barely breathe. What the hell do we do now? We are lost.* Nigel would be the one to help me get back to our cave when we would go out to explore. We have lost our group, we are injured, and worst off, do not know what has happened.

I make a mud pile the shape of a small tub to lay around and over Thomas. I am not sure if he will end up losing his leg, but it looks like he will. We are both lucky to be alive at this point. If the Rotter we left behind did not pass out from losing so much blood, all of those creatures would have chased after us.

"Where are we?" Thomas asks, regaining consciousness. "You saved my life, Duke."

"You saved your own life, by staying alive. I just carried you." I state. "But don't mention it. I'm your wingman, right?"

"Yeah. I guess that Rotter Amos didn't have one." Thomas smirks in response. "It looks like he was the set up to the sacrifice."

"What in the realm are you talking about?" I joke back. "And how did you know his name was Amos?" I do not know what in hell he is talking about now. First, the other man hit on the damn head, and now Thomas is the one talking crazy.

"I don't know if that was what his real name is, but that is what they called him in the curfews." Thomas clarifies. The curfews are the times most of the Rotters turn in for the night to avoid the predators in the Rapture. Many of them get together with all of the other Rotters, even those who do not go to the sun-times, and they gossip about the realms. Thomas goes on to explain, "Amos is to be the one they choose to set up for Predeterminism, as a sacrifice to the spirits, if we were to encounter any Angels on the way to sun-times."

"Are you saying they had someone predetermine Amos's death, just to sacrifice him? Well, this means that Amos's attacker tried to kill him." All of the information I am programming into memory. Not only do I have a photographic mind, but I also could not forget what had just happened to us. "Why would they set up someone to think of killing Amos, all to summon the Angels?"

The ground violently shakes just as Thomas begins to respond, with branches from the nearby trees discarding harden chemical dust. The clouds darken to shape the patterns of universal life, with an array of lightning storms inside of them. All of the gravel, dying tree branches and debris head towards the center of the storm, in the direction we came from miles away. Above the clouds form a pattern of lightning in distinctively connected shapes we can hardly make out. The winds scream in reverse crescendos of piercing whistles, with a high pitch tone that begins to bleed out my infected ear.

"It's one of them transitioning. I knew it was coming!" Thomas yells out frantic. I assume he has heard of the transitional phase of the Angelic realm into another dimension. These spiritly demonic Angels use a dimensional portal, each one of them uniquely transformed, to travel through space and the cosmos. I quickly learn the patterns of the lightning sequence and count the number of booming sounds. To my calculations, this event took place approximately one hundred meters from where we left the Rotter to die.

The essence of the sky and winds calm, as the clouds thicken not allowing any visibility. The only sounds I can hear are Thomas trembling in fear, hiding under his mud patch. Without warning, I hear seven firework looking bursts in the sky, as the thick clouds cut open an oval passage. A bullhorn smoke vortex comes down out of the firmament, widening towards the terrain, with outer light purple rings. This is the materials used to produce the portals and transition of the Angelic Realm. The demon spirit violently descends through the purplish smoke phenomenal, into the atmosphere. It is too far in the distance to make out the distortive features from our position.

"The Angel is retrieving the Rotter's sacrifice. The Violent is going after the Rotter who attacked Amos." I proclaim aloud. A Violent Angel is one who cast down with a purple hue and is notoriously evil in nature. The Rotters, who plotted against whoever attacked Amos, would not be within miles of a descending Angel. They must have tied up the attacker to leave for the demon spirit to find. The chemistry and kinematic energy, which produce the Violent Angel, suddenly reverse upward into the sky, and a flash of light ascends through the purple smoke. A flailing body emerges from the earth immediately behind and slowly disappears, as the clouds collapse closing in the sky.

"Oh my God. Christ. What was that, and what did you say? Did you call that thing a Violent Angel?" Thomas sputters.

"Don't worry about it. The Angel is gone now. We have bigger things to deal with, Thomas." I calmingly state to him. I can see one million questions on his puzzled muddy face arise. There is no sign of the sun, and there is not a single person or creature around us for miles. I manage to find a dense hole and remove enough debris to place Thomas inside of it. I start a small fire a few feet away from us and gather up as many insects as I can for us to cook. This will be a temporary shelter for us until I can get my transition back into the new world. As for Thomas, he will likely die soon.

Back in the new world, you can enjoy the sounds of birds through the sky sing to one another. Being here in the Rapture world, the sounds of the creatures here are of danger and fear. Why even bother to look behind me anymore? I have not heard a sound or seen any movement at all from Thomas. To be honest, his is not going to make it out alive. Does everyone who ends up dealing with me die? It is funny for me when I think about it- not that everyone ends up dying around me. You ever think to yourself, does a person know they may end up dying today? Does someone wake up in the morning, and say to oneself, *this is a great day to end up six feet under*? Asking somebody about my logic with this topic always made me feel weird. People have a hard time, as it is to understand my logic. If I could ask that question to people, I would. At least I would know if they end up dead, they were up for it at the beginning.

The insects crawling the insides of Thomas's eyes prevents him from seeing his severed leg. This is not going as planned. I can use the rest of Thomas's water and food for me to survive for now. I give the water positive thoughts for it to remain purified after what has taken place. I must give blessing and prayers over what I have left, keeping my sanity. *I have to get back to the mission.* So, who am I, and how did I end up in a hole next to a dying man, away from the new world, here in this realm? Well, it is more complexing than volunteering to the Global Council to prevent, Predeterminism. The only thing I can do now at this point reflects back to how I got here. Why did I volunteer to come to this realm in the first place? What was I doing back in the new world? I recall the recent days before all of what has supervened. Back in the new world.

3

JUNE 28th, 2052

Shadows from the street lamps grow, as each citizen travels to their destination, constantly with their heads tilted up towards the skies. It is several days before me reporting to the 6th realm as a volunteer and patches of clouds flash with lightning at this hour of the night, alluding to the approaching limitations. Being out in the streets after the curfew is like being out during a sacrificial purification. Mind-stalks use of chants, sorcerers who offer channeling, new world priests, and thousands of more Seers, Oracles, and Prophesiers flood the streets. There are hundreds of underground sects and cults.

The Global Councils of each Nation oversee a centralized planet of faith-citizens, in hopes to bring order to obey the Gods. Many, who speculate about the souls of the earth, oppose the warnings of the Global Council and turn to the underground for answers. Young people attempt to join various sects in the streets of the new world to avoid becoming what they deem, 'Faith slave-citizens.' Underground organizations have developed and raised leaders of the anti-established Global Councils across the planet. These underground organizations educate about the deadly manipulations of the Elite. Much to the surprise of the population the underground safeguards and guide many stray children with spiritual knowledge and ultimate protection. Faith-citizens however, do not risk losing a child to the underground occult. The future generations are the primary focus of many people.

One by one, the sound of heels falling down on the payment echoes closer and closer. At the beginning of a dead end ally, a stray cat runs after a rotting apple a young girl drops out of a pocket while running to escape her older guardian sibling. Two mice ambush out from a trash can, chasing the stray cat into a nearby abandon building, alerting the brother who turns to see his sister is missing.

The young girl runs a distance away, yielding to catch her breath. Out of an inside sleeve patched together from fibers, the girl pulls out a letter with the directions to a nearby safe point. She comes next to a brick wall covered with huge spider webs and leans against it to support herself. Snatching the webs from her long hair, the girl glances up to see if anyone witnesses, in a dark underground staircase. Her elbows tremble beating against the wall as she quietly reads out.

"To whoever is in possession of this document currently, if you are unauthorized to read this notice, it may be too late, for it has been laced with chemicals as part of the security measures for our organization. If you were selected to be in possession of this material, then you are safe, and will know of the containing chemicals used and soon will have a knowledge of the next steps to take after you read this document."

The red-inked paragraph on the top of the letter is to prevent the information from being place around to the wrong people. She continues. "This is a message invite only, from the Leaders Union Underground Network. The L.U.U.N will be conducting interviews tonight only at a hidden location. After the first 15 minutes of the next beginning storm during this evening's curfew, possible new recruits shall meet in the unknown coordinates which will be giving shortly."

Before the young girl can go on to the next sentence, she hears a beeping distress signal come from under the bottom of her pant leg. A flickering red light alerts her that she has a locator placed on by her sibling, without her knowledge. "What the heck?" Sliding down the wall, she falls to her butt and crosses her leg on her knees to remove the device. "I hate him. I can never do anything!"

She realizes that she cannot detach the item and would not dare run around without any pants. Her head backs against the wall. A spider falls into her hair and runs along the side of her cheeks. She trembles in silence, watching the spider climb down past her chest. Sliding up the wall with her back, she quickly turns around to smash the insect with her chest against the bricks. Tears puddle from her face as she covers her voice not to cause anyone to find her location. She falls to her knees and walks up the staircase on all fours, knocking over a glass jar. Leaning back to catch the bottle after several bounces, she tumbles down the steps cutting her hand from the broken glass.

"Ouch. Ugh, no." She cries out. "I have to get out of here before my brother comes." A shard of broken glass helps her cut the pant leg to leave behind the tracking device, and she darts up the stairs. She is a fourteen-year-old girl from Japan named Aiko. Her parents moved to Japan after the wars and killed by conventional new world disasters. The only family left is her protector whom she calls her brother, Lon.

Aiko makes it two blocks and trips into a stockpile of cardboard boxes, startled by the midnight Sirens. The streets across the joint populated nations standing integrated with Predeterminism technologies, and monitoring systems, including intercoms, telecommunications, and 100 feet poles hosting large arena sized monitor speakers. The biggest nations in the old world remain, while each of the harboring smaller countries integrated into them. The first announcement of the lockouts echoes across the world from city to city 15 minutes before their respected time zones, where each faith-citizens resides. The only call of the night prompts through the Sirens as follows:

'Attention faith-citizens of the new world. You will have 15 minutes after this announcement to return to your homes due to the limitations. Those that do not comply and continue to break the laws will be monitored and obtained by the authorities. You will not go to any courts, you will not see any judges, and you will be committed to the Rapture world. Those that do not comply and continue to break the laws will not be protected by Predeterminism, if you commit a murder or if you preconceive thoughts of death. You are left to the Judgement of the Angelic realm during these curfews. The Global Council has warned you, and you will not be protected. For your own protection, do as you are told at this time and return to your homes. This is the only way you will be protected with Predeterminism, and to remain a faith-citizen. The limitation will be over at sunrise. Please think highly of others and remain legally determine. Thank you for being a giving faith-citizen.'

The end of the Sirens passes through the habitats of the populated planet, through each time zone accordingly. By the end of the announcements, Aiko remains beneath the pile of cardboard bleeding and rattled. Pulling her emotions inside, she takes a deep breath to focus on her mission. Bunched under her is a yellow stained paper.

"I wouldn't wrap your hand up with that if I were you, tiny one." A gray voice blows directly behind her sweaty hair.

"Who is there?" Screaming out, she rolls off the cardboard and turns back on all fours with fear. The largest piece of cardboard is under the other pieces. A huge gust of winds lifts the flat cardboard away down the sidewalk to reveal an old and disgusting looking man. His clothes halfway stay on his frame, and his hair is cover with the filth of the streets.

"This is I; I am the one who saves you. My name is Fortress." He stumbles forward to his feet. "Please, do not draw any more attention to yourself by running away." Before Aiko can make a sound, the man swipes his arm causing a huge gust of wind to cover her whole body with several large pieces of newspaper and cardboard.

"Who the hell are you speaking through now, old man? Let me guess; you can see my Mother from the dead." A giant man presents himself from behind Fortress, knocking him to the ground. "Stay off of this street!" Fortress reaches to his feet to look back for the young girl. There is one shoe visible and a pile of newspaper trembling to his amusement. The huge man disappears down the shadows destroying inanimate objects in his path.

Fortress makes his way over to Aiko as a gust of wind removes the newspapers from her body. Visibly shaken and scared half to death, Aiko faints and lays on the ground innocently.

The night has just begun, and the majority of faith citizens have scattered to their homes forewarned. The new world becomes night and day after the curfews start. For the short and few hours in the limitations, much is underground and unseen. The birds in the sky echo through the cities. The remaining citizens who have nowhere to go struggle to find the underground cities. Not all of the people in the streets can join the organizations and left to fend for themselves. Few faith citizens stay out and offer food and water to those that are without. However, eventually, the faith citizens return to their homes within a few minutes after the beginning of the Sirens for their own protection. This is the new world.

4

THE UNDERGROUND WORLD is dark and threatening. A separate territory hosts the religious believers outside of the consciousness of faith-citizens. Those who manage to do well in the underground world find their calling before crossing over. Some say that the underground world is the only thing in between the new world and the Rapture realms.

"Are you sure you can trust him? What is taking so long?" Lon asks.

"Don't worry; your sister is fine," I try to reassure. "Fortress will make sure she gets to us safely. We need you to go and check on the preparations for the rest of the recruits."

The wind levels below the cities in silence after the first hour in the curfews. The lights are dim. The only sounds are aftershocks below the earth and volatile explosions. Most of the people left in the street are of no use to anyone; they are what the world considers, vegetable trays. The Global Council has deemed their minds empty and therefore have no use to produce faith to the God Realm, or so they believe.

Pass a deserted block of unemployed connected complex buildings leads to an old Masonic temple inside of Narian, Scotland. The outside of the temple's gothic style encased with wilting vines. A masses colony of crows protects the entrance doors. Inside the doors is the tunnel to an underground network. Entering a sect of the underground is a challenging deal to accomplish for the people of this planet unless you are a child or secretly selected. I had many dealing with underground leaders and come as I please, connecting through both worlds. Many of the leaders view me as the open gateway to the global world and the underground, I, on the other hand, work on no one's side.

A small crowd gathers in an outer courtyard next to a statue park that is the nostalgia of an ancient terrorizing ritual. The underground host talented artists who create images, statues, coal paintings and more, making it their living for survival. However, the new world has a unified standard for currency and trade- these commorancies resort to their own means. A bruised faced woman projects her voice among the listeners:

"This night we raise up our children's right to breathe the air of The Great Truth. No man shall hold dignity in destroying the future abilities to the earth. The Gods of men and women have no mercy to offer validity of their given proof. Also, these demons are man's creation controlling the minds at first birth. We do not believe in the lesser of evils plan to unify us against the powers. The casting of Souls shows us how cruel and dependent the heavens be. Come one and all to the union of The Deliverance to challenge…"

Shouts of angry people echo, "Sit down shrew; no one wants to hear you."

"You deserve to be departed in a Rapture."

"You are an evil spy spent by the Elite."

"Set her up to be a sacrifice."

"We have our freedoms here."

Just as the crowds begin to rally to the woman speaking on the edge of a gargoyle statue, two large hands grab both her feet and knees, bringing her to the ground. She groans, turns to her back, laying on the pavement to see two security watchers of the underground lift her up to her feet. "We thought we kicked you out of here, evil old Harridan." They laugh.

"What type of fake prophet has to minister to the underground, indeed?"

"How about you take your book and your Gods to the top and spill your lies there? Go and preach to the faith citizens." He commands. The Watchers hold the woman in the air and converse between each other.

"How do you think she was able to sneak in this time? Maybe she has a secret spell that her believers pray for, to rapture through the gates."

"That's not how it works," The second guard says. "Their Messiah has to come down first and deliver them to the kingdom of heaven. The problem is, heaven has come down, and the Elite was their Messiah. Or maybe she practices out of a Kabbalah ritual?"

"Enough, enough already. Place her down. We have more important things to accomplish." The two Watchmen are surprised to see Lon standing behind them with his double barrel sawn off shotgun pointed at them. His hand grabs the head watcher's arm, and the old woman slowly lowered from the interrogation. The Abbess runs off, and the two Watchers immediately look upwards toward the sky. "Do you two think I have shit for brains? Now, let's go." Lon leads his two henchmen watchers to the hidden locations to gather the new recruits converting from faith-citizens.

The reasons for my being in both the underground and the new world are both personal and business. Part of me believes that for the people in the underground to understand what is happening in the Global Council, they have to hear the truth from me. No one here knows what I do or who I really am. That is except for one of the leaders, who I hope will help lead us to the source of this world. The power behind the deception.

"Come with me. We have to leave now. Hurry!" I plead to Lon. I start trailing behind to redirect him off his path.

"Romas? This is the fastest route back up to…"

"I know but…, just trust me. I sense an anomaly." The dry leaves brush off my feet as we head in the opposite direction. The sky above cracks, echoing through the crowds of the statue park. A dark man with an unseen face, wearing a black trench coat, turns behind the crowd just as I look back. I continue to run to reach the new world at a steady pace.

"How do you do that?" Lon stops behind us, leaning on an abandon building gate. "How do you know what is going on?"

"If I told you, you wouldn't stop asking me questions."

"Well, tell me where my sister is and tell me what's going on?" He takes his shotgun to his side. I stop and slowly walk back.

"I know you may want me to feel as if you brought upon that anomaly back there, by placing your gun to your followers. Nevertheless, you and I know you are not dumb enough to think about killing anyone. Especially, when you are worried about protecting your little sister." I pick up a large rock and aim it in his direction. In a fluid motion, I grasp the massive rock from my side with both hands and cast it towards Lon. "You should move!" The wooden gate bears a huge hole from the stone I threw missing Lon's head.

"Goddam, you jerk!" He dusts off the infected leafs and branches from the ground off his coat.

"If that were true, then next time I won't say anything, now will I?" I pull up a rusted metal pole and burst the rest of the hole open. The two watchmen and I break our way through the wooden gate and commence to enter the building as Lon picks himself off the ground, apparently still aggravated. "Let's make this short and sweet. We don't have much time to play Jeopardy." I turn back to help him to his feet, and we walk through the abandoned building.

5

THE BUILDING RUINED old and full of paintings. The courtyard was a museum that was a Scottish tourist attraction in the early 21st century. It was no comparison to the Detroit Masonic Temple in the United States, at only half the size, which converted into a faith-worshiping center to the God realm. The abandoned temple nearly destroyed from the chaotic global cabal.

We enter into the building climbing over fallen bricks and around tumbled walls. I instruct the watchers to stay up front and stand guard as I take Lon down a dark hallway. We reach a room with a collapsed ceiling, shining in a yellow spotted moon.

"This is good enough. I have something I would like to show you." I place my hand on Lon's shoulder and sit him down on top of a floored panel. "After this, just promise never to repeat what you were told."

"By the way, things are going, I may not make it alive that long. But, you have my word" He places his shotgun down. "I'm not sure if I want to hear this." Lon is an interesting person to me. He declines to become a leader of any top underground organizations. He once even turned down the opportunity to join the Global Council. His parents were humanitarians, who legally made it possible to adopt over one hundred children during the wars. His parents did not live to see the coming of the Angelic realm, however. All but one of their children were lost. His sister was the only one he could save. Aiko.

Protecting his sister was his only purpose in life, besides fighting the corrupt laws outside of the God Realm that the council has created. Managing to keep his secrets from his sister about the underground was easy. The trusty shotgun would put many holes in those who tried to do them harm, and Lon knew that as long as he had no intent to kill, he would be protected from a Rapture. I take a few steps away from Lon and detach a harness from my back. Opening up my bag, I display the contents I had with me the whole time. I press a series of codes and place my fingerprints on a device, which shows a hologram that bounces off particles through the darkness.

"This is what is known as, a monitor alertus. The alertus is a portable Predeterminism device used by monitors to conduct surveillance through the new world." A crystal hologram image displays his two men out front awaiting our return in real time.

"Do you mean to tell me that... you're a Monitor?" Looking down at his shotgun, "It all makes sense now. I guess I should have known." Before he could say another word, the device flashes to display his sister at the main base of the L.U.U.N. Aiko is well taken care of and has been through the introduction of the underground, along with several other recruits. I revert to the courtyard. The alertus is now displaying the guards' converse. Projecting a light blue shadowed hologram across the room, I pace inside of my thoughts before I speak. The time is now, right here.

"Many decades ago, the intellects decided that we needed to search into the cosmos to uncover the universe. Scientists and researchers spent thousands of hours and trillions of dollars to find answers to the universe, which was already here in this world. The globalist, Elite, and the scientific world were not satisfied with the fact that ancient civilizations may have been able to uncover truths, which we were not willing to accept. Therefore, we allowed them to rewrite our history and deceive us through manipulation, science, and religion.

"Yet, no one was willing to say that we live inside of what this universe has created. It is but only our interpretation of what we are prepared to accept and believe. The first truth that we must learn to appreciate is that there is no such thing as truth- dealing with science. Secondly, there is no such thing as good and evil- dealing with religion. And lastly, the spirit is the sustainable energy of the universe, and we must not destroy this power." I realize that Lon is suffering from his lengthy plight. The last thing he wants to hear is preaching the universe and explaining my belief system.

I continue. "Listen. Let us say that no one knows the answers. No one from the ancient civilizations, none of the most renowned philosophers or prophets, and none of the most brilliant scholars or scientist. Out of all of these individual sources that we can turn to, the one thing that holds all of the answers and never changes is the spirit."

"But, tell me, Romas, what does that have to do with why we are here? The only spirits I see floating around in this world are the evil one's, who are trying to take over, or the demons who are trying to take souls."

"You are exactly right. The only ones that you see." I take my fingers and reposition them on the alertus. Pressing several sequences, I display an historical event from 2018. The alertus hologram recounts events of the delivery of The James Webb telescope. "We were people who believed that we could be capable of God or see what God can do. The man has been deliberate in attempting to find answers in space. After developing the most advanced technological engineering equipment we could, these scientists have still failed. The telescope did not live up to expectations, and the space community was left to go back to the drawing board."

Standing to his feet, Lon gets up close to have a better view. "But I thought that the telescope was deployed in space as planned? We seen and learned new discovers for the first time in history. Look, for the sake of time, please explain what it is you are talking about. If you can, skip any euphuistic theology." It was the first sign of a smile I saw from Lon.

We share an uplifting smile. "I will try my best. Take the last statement you said for instance. You said, for the first time in history we have learned new discoveries. Moreover, for the science community, there lies the dilemma inside of the paradox.

"The James Webb telescope was able to peer farther back into time than Hubble was capable of doing, in an attempt to know what happened to the universe after the so-called Big Bang. Now, do not misunderstand me when I do believe it is important to understand how stars and galaxies were formed. We as humans can only understand based upon our perception. What about explaining and understand what the Big Bang theory is first? After all, it is much easier to say that there was darkness, and out of the darkness, there was light." From what I can tell, Lon is challenging my logic inside his head.

"Are you saying that we need to concentrate on what or who created the light in the first place?" He states. With both hands falling from the air to his side, he turns around to see images from space. He goes on to continue, "I see where you are going with this. It is easy to say that there was a big bang on one side and that it God who creates the world on the other. Still, no one can explain where the energy came from in the first place."

Immediately after his thoughts, the hologram hosts an array of mind-blowing illustrations and images from past and present theologies, scientific equations and philosophical theories. The most wondrously beautiful depictions of heaven and the universe emulate throughout the perforating ruins. Stammering with awe, Lon trips against the side of his shotgun, sending out a lucky shot. The blast echoes down the crumbling hall unpredicted, surprising the watchers out front. Arising from a dust covering flooring, hair full of vermin feces, Lon punches up. More surprised than what is occurring, he turns to see my finger pointing directly at him.

"You create the energy." After my conclusion, the hologram ends. My hand extends to catch the Alertus in midair, as its anti-gravity hovering system shuts off. I look down at Lon to see a bewildered expression. My hands vibrate with escaping multi-flashing lights coming from the device. I sharply store the Alertus hearing a desperate page from the Watchmen entering the corridor.

"They must have been aroused by the gun shots." He turns back to retrieve his weapon.

With a concerned look on my face, I place my hand on his shoulder, "Not exactly. Come on; we have to go. Now!"

I begin to sense a change occurring. I realize that I can tell when there is a buildup of kinetic energy around me. Almost as if there is a little voice in my head going off like a triggering alarm. I often have heard voices in my head since my childhood. Good and bad. The real sounds were the ones I credit protecting me as a runaway. The bad voices were there to keep me alive as well. It was the reason I was able to mislead and deceive my way through the streets of life. Most people that I encountered were impressed that I was able to take care of myself. People would often praise about my street smarts. It was the voices in my head.

Now I sense danger. It is the same intense feeling I had back when I first caught up with Lon and his Watchmen. The dust particles in the room are beginning to float upward, like helium. Throughout the hallways and into each room, you can hear a little clatter of cheap china tea cups rattling off saucers. The ground silently shakes slow, yet noticeably, far too quiet and steady however to be an earthquake.

6

THERE COMES A TIME when you must stand for what you believe in, command your positions, firmly holding your ground. The world consumes weakness. The strongest not only survive, but they also thrive. Then, there are times when you need to run like hell.

Gathering our equipment in a hurry, we go to join the other two men in the dark banquet hall, filled with huge spider webs we have to chop down with blades. The windows clunk apart in a vibrating rumble. Several rusted dining tables fall down. We look up to witness multitudes of bats soar through the huge opening that once was a structure. From a horror movie scene, the elegant absence of the ceiling filled with flying bats and echoed shrieks.

"Is this what I think it is? Please, tell me this is an evil dream." The lead watcher runs up to us with fear, trembling as he finally reaches us.

"Where is your partner," With a puzzled look on Lon's face, "why did you split up?"

"It is maybe too late for him. The spirits don't come here by mistake." I try to distract their attention away from the hall entrance. "It isn't much else we can do if we tried. No one heard any sounds outside, so that means it can only be one type of Angel."

"So let's go back and help him!" I grab Lon by his jacket and stop him from running off. "What are you doing?" He turns back to look at me.

"We need to leave now. Your Watchman will more than likely try to defend himself."

"Why would he do that Romas? There is a demon out there."

"If you keep asking questions, you will find out. An Angel who makes no sound when it transitions is a shifter. They are able to take on any form that they please. These Angels are known to draw their victims in, for pleasure upon a Rapture, if you could say." I lead the remaining two men down the corridor. I open my bag to view the case that I have stated, making sure not to expose the alertus. Running into dead ends and hidden rooms, we hurdle out an opening through a wall. The only place we have not been, up. We jump over concrete to the stairwell, across two or three missing steps, ascending upward to the second level.

Broken tiles fall from a distance leap between three levels as Lon grabs along the railing to hang in the air. The staircase trembles with thunder blasts leaving Lon desperately hanging on between myself, and the other side of the missing steps. By this time, the temple is full of carbon and swirling dust. As I try to reach for Lon's arm, I see the silhouette of the missing Watchman, frozen below us, just inside a doorway. I grasp onto the railing and extend my leg out for Lon to hold onto. The second guard scales the side of the wall with his fingertips right behind me.

I am the only person who has attention below, as I cut my eyes beneath our current predicament. "Now is not the best time to hang on the side of the wall, my friend."

"You are going to have to do more than just give me your leg Romas." The only parts of Lon's body I can see is from the breastplate up, pulling himself on the stairs, slowly. Lon has his elbows extended locked, trying to yank upwards. The other Watchmen losses his grip on one hand to the rails and now dangles in the air as well. I turn back my attention downstairs to witness a pale white/light blue hue reflect off the guard's silhouette.

Seeming to levitate forward off the ground, I look down to notice the missing guard draws towards the voice of a young woman inside a room. I am now the only person who is conscious of the events including the captive. From the room below, a young female rhythm's out the name of the guard hanging on the steps next to me. The man suddenly tilts himself sideways suspended in a waft of air, looking to the ground in dread. He then releases his grip and thunderbolts, snapping both his ankles from the fall. Like in a movie scene, his screams of agony belt across our eardrums as we witness the guard's body slung along the floor by an invisible force. The screams yield faintly away as the payment levels out with dense fog.

Reaching back to my feet, I extend my arms to grab for Lon. At the same time, Lon lifts up towards me, his gun strap snaps throwing the weapon in a decent. Negligence provokes his reaction to catching the shotgun, which causes him to lose his grip. Flash. He falls into the fog and disappears before my eyes.

"Lon… no!" A strong gust of air presses me up and over the missing steps, and I climb to the second floor with remorse. "God damn. What the hell just happened?" Trying to realize what has taken place; I run through the temple second level and manage to withstand the crumbling building. Passing a room on my right, I grab the doorway to slow me down. I notice several tree branches has protruded through the wall over time and flee down the shredded bark to the ground below. I do not look back. Why would I need to turn around now? As I continue to belt down the road out of the building's vicinity, the top of the temple explodes into pieces. I cannot tell which direction the fluorescent light begins or ends heaven or earth.

Hesitant to turn around, I leap over obstructions and debris, which the winds consume back in the direction I escape. I know that the Angel is departing with my friends. Soon as I open my bag to view the Alertus, a strong gust of wind passes me over a sinkhole, causing my device to venture down into the earth below. After landing, one foot after the other, my pace increases by two times. The impending sounds of the Rapture grow faint as I distance myself from the horrid divinity. For the next two miles, I run until I reach a safe haven, away from the devastation in the underground that I have witnessed. The Curfews are over soon. I have to send a communication to the leaders and continue.

"I will find you, my friend." Thoughts of Lon resonate in my mind. My journey must proceed the first sunlight onward from here. I walk through shadows and ill thoughts.

I make it back out from the underground. This is what happens with reality. It does not matter the state of mind or consciousness you are in, or world you believe yourself to be apart. The reality is the truth behind all of the ideas you place in your mind to change your perception for the better. It does not matter what you believe or deceives you to think. The reality is an auction, and the truth of it goes to the highest bidder- meaning that everyone disregards the lowest bids and focuses on the element's new owner.

Birds do not sing now afraid of the presence of predators, and demons. There is a new moon opposite of the sunrise. The illuminated birch trees breed the sky along with bees. The global Elite successfully cloned Diploid (generated) eggs, which produce female bee offspring. Hundreds of bees fall out of the heavens due to the atmosphere each day. The ones that stay alive pollenate. Even when we try to make things in life go right, they go wrong. Lon was a right that went wrong. I remain in the coastline and cut through the forest. As I continue across the woods to home, I still cannot understand what had taken place at the temple. *Where did this Angel come from and why?* The only conclusion that I can come to is the spirits are after me.

7

THE ANNOUNCEMENT of the morning day prompts through the Sirens as follows:

'Attention faith-citizens of the new world. You have approximately 15 minutes until the Curfews lifted for this day, the possible day of the 29th, June 2052. Please obey all governing law sanctioned by the Global Council, ordained of the God realm. If you do not comply, you will be subjected to Predeterminism or worst, Rapture. We as faith-citizens of this newly transitioned world produced to us by the Gods are their humble servants. The faith citizen's obligation and committal that will help keep our planet safe. Please think highly of others and remain legally determine. Thank you for being a giving faith-citizen.'

Shaken, to say the least, as I open my door. Several turning combinations later, the locks give me a false security inside the barrier. I made it home. My report for work, tomorrow about what has accrued, will be brutal. The best way to get around that is to put it off until next Friday. Somethings here in the new world stay the same. Right now, I do not know what is more frustrating; I lost an Alertus device, the Angelic realm is after me, or I caused Lon to Raptured. I drop down to my knees to cry. Pretending as if I misplaced something, I search around the floor to realize that I am a monitor, and no one is watching *me*. At least I think.

Coffee only takes a few seconds to make. I open a foil package that has a sugar-sized brown cube inside. Placing the cube in the water causes the chemicals inside to heat to temperature and release the coffee flavor. I rush off to retrieve my backup device. With a few inputs on the instrument, I find myself going back into the past. I remember the first day I physically encountered Lon. He had no idea I had been watching him for weeks. I program the alertus backup that I have to recall the events on this day.

Life has a strange way of continuing even when many face suffrage and persecution. This day was several years before the overthrowing powers, new world Elite, and doomsayers had declared war. Aiko is in her third soccer game, and Lon is there to cheer her on. The air is a mist, and the children love it. I sit a few seats above Lon on the bleachers behind. There are parents, family members and friends cheering on the youth. It is only Lon and Aiko. The chilled bench has built up moisture next to the only vacant spot that is on his right. He offers his seat to a stunning woman who seems to be out of sitting options. Her hair is wet and long. The backside of her jumpsuit is dry, her shoulders bare- showery. Unpretentiousness surrounds her beauty with a light of effervescence over her head. She seems to have come right out of the heaven. Beautiful.

"Please, have a seat here, Miss." The towel to dry off his sister placed on the bench.

"Why, thank you." Smiles exchange between them. I am too far away to hear the *converspering* they have, and to what I can tell, it is going well. I see a gleam of passion in the eyes of Lon and this woman. Sincerity. The two hold only wind in between them and little light. *Love at first sight?* I have witnessed this before. It is genuine. The amount of energy two people shares when there is love, at first sight, is superior to anything else. Every inch of sound vibration disappears away, and only the two hear each other's voices. The next world surrounding the pair goes as in a movie, leaving them alone in a white incandescent room. Time stands still, and each of the two can hear every breath the other takes simultaneously.

Nevertheless, love, at first sight, is hard, complicated, and can be dangerous. Eventually, the world that is around the two will come back in. The two will soon find out that they are not in love with each other. They have shared spiritual intimacy. Soon they will realize that unless they never go apart, they can never hold on to this spiritual ecstasy. Being in love is planned and deliberate. Experiences of love at first sight, are temporary and universally exquisite, unparalleled. No two other beings can share this same experience, for each individual spirit has embraced the others energy as their own. Also, for this reason, no other persons outside these two can accept this or understand. Lon and this mysterious woman hold hands and wonder helplessly into each other's eyes. The world cannot know. The entire crowd feels atmospherical energy.

Jealousy overcomes an arrogant man nearby. He and his counterpart approach the couple with disregard of their nature. The larger of the two assailants move a person sitting next to the woman. The man grabs her hand away to woe. Lon pops up off his seat to comfort the man, to see his counterpart on the left side jump on the bleachers, cocking back his arm. The larger man snatches the fearful woman away by her arm as on goers look with amazement. The man wraps his arms around her trembling shoulders as she looks back at Lon in fear.

Eyes wide with a face full on grin, I reach for my snacks and refreshments. I have no idea that I was in for multiple forms of entertainment on that evening. Soon as I kick my feet up upon the bleachers, Lon couples the towel at both ends and takes the second man's legs from him in mid swing. His head bounces off the bleachers like a soccer ball, as cheers and screams fill the field. I make out Lon from the fleeing crowd in the middle of the field. The relentless heathen, who has taken the woman, squares up to throw a desperate hail maker at Lon, missing. Lon splits down the perpetrator with ease in a flash.

By this time security has control of the situation, Aiko left with tears streaming down her face as her Brother placed in handcuffs. The two offenders attended to by the medical staff, and I cannot stop laughing, historically. At this point, I am wondering the same thing almost every other person is. *Where is the woman?* After the crowd disperses, I could not place her, as if she disappeared into thin air. With this being years before I became a monitor and the Predeterminism program launch, I have no way of finding her. Just as always, a static set of lines obscures the hologram on the alertus as I try to display the location of this mystery woman. This is the same type of anomaly as was in the temple.

"Ouch. Dammit!" I lose my train of thought after burning my lips from taking a sip of coffee. *If I had not been so close to Lon, then none of this would have happened.* I never bring up the past story of the woman to Lon. He has been through enough in his life.

Life has a mystical virtuosity to it. How often we think, *if it were not for 'A' happening, then I would have never experienced 'B.'* Philosophy principles of causation. One of our base modules in Predeterminism. The mind works, based on interpretational reactions. How do we, prevent 'A' forming probability? What do I know? It is as if I am reading the job description for my position at work aloud when I think.

Maybe the Global Council created the system to stop a predisposition to doing harm to others, but that does little to prevent a reaction to purposely-created situations, which invoke the trigger. The new world is full with criminals who cause the destruction of others through mind manipulation.

I am way off tangent now.

I have to come to grasp with why I am here, what is my purpose in life. These Angels of Darkness may not be evil. The spiritual beings could be Angels, sent down by the Gods to protect us from evil.

I have a hard time understanding evil in itself. I often ask myself questions about the subject. A furious animal attacking someone's pet is wrong in the past; this type of nature deemed evil as such. However, now in the new world, certain animals carry diseases that kill humans. The diseased animals have migrated across the planet and repopulated, leaving the furious creatures attacks on them acceptable and no longer evil today.

Since the beginning of the creation of duality, the interpretation of right and wrong has changed through the centuries. *So then, are these spiritual beings or Angels, good or bad?* Whatever the understanding of what they are, I now know what my mission is? To find out the answers. The alertus device interrupts my train of thought. A message indicating some new protocols implemented at work next week pulls up. *Why do I get distracted from deep thoughts? It never fails.*

There are some inventions or products that the underground has produced that help in life in the new world. I turn down the hallway to my closet. The glowing light from my candles dances shadows along my walls as I pass by. Just below the ceiling is a long electronic strip that scans my movements powered by device recognition software.

A red line follows my movements down the hall and forms a grid on my closet door in front of me. After a quick scan, the door automatically opens where I place all of the items I collect in the underground for future analysis. Most of all the elements in the underground sell on the black market and are illegal to possess for regular faith-citizens. As a monitor, I have the authority to observe them and report these items to the Global Council.

There has to be an article to help me understand why I have become unbalanced with my thoughts. Back in the underground, I overheard a Fakir explain the unstable nature of our bodies may be one cause of distractions we receive from our relative states. At first, I thought he was only trying to sell his invention, but I decided to research into it some more.

Inside the dark closet illuminated by a dim red light, I start to search for an item known as the Aquatic imploder. The imploder was similar to those a few decades ago, but with added elements, predecessors did not include spirituality. The people of the new world have become more in tune with spirituality and the engineers of the new Imploders introduced, the power of the operative spoken word.

The instructions to the device read as follows:

[The Aquatic imploder engineered to rebalance your inner spirituality, realigning you once again to the universal cosmos. Correctly used, the imploder shall help you reach a clearer atonement to help you focus on these dark times. First, fill the device with water, after giving the water a thorough blessing. The device powered by speech only will work after stating the exact commands:

'I give thanks to my spiritual intuition today, for giving me the divine knowledge to rebalance my being. Blessed are the impurities in this water, which are forgiving and allowed to release freely. I Am thankful; I Am blessed, and I Am life.'

You have successfully prepared the water for consumption. You may now drink.]

I finish the rest of my imploded water and go into a deep meditative state of consciousness. My eyes are light, as they close with my head tilted up to the ceiling. An imprint of my pupil's form in the darkness on the inside of my eyelids. The image has a yellow silhouette with darkly spotted cell organisms inside. My mind vividly flashes scenes of the spiritual beings, from the previous encounters. I can hear the screams of my party echo. I see the horrid looks on their faces as the spirits cast into the atmosphere and appeal before us. Now, instead of Lon and his men taken by the Angelic beings, I am the one raptured.

My vision becomes gray and cloudy. A high pitch inside my ears rings. A shield protects me from

Angel's grasp. My eyes close and I hear words spoken aloud to the demons. What are these words? The cadence retracts the Angels away from me back into the heavens. As I open my eyes, I realize that some time has passed, and I am complete restored. I look back down at the imploder. *This has to have some fantasies in here.* With a loss for words. Are the answers in this spoken word? I spend the rest of my day researching my hypothesis before I head to sleep.

8

THE NEXT MORNING, I take my cloth shoes off and walk to the kitchen. The lights illuminate my path as I continue to pass my meditation sanctuary. My vibrations channel an orange hue and relaxing alpha waves play in the background for concentration. The constant echo sound of a horse trout emphasizes in a pattern underneath the melodic tones. This is a ritual for me every night that I spend at home.

A child raised by Priests and Nuns has its upsides. Back in Ecuador, many years ago, I studied the significance of eating the correct way. *Beep*. The sound of my steam producer notifies me that my insect, seaweed, and algae burger are prepared to eat. I not only praise my meal; I bless it with an eternal gratitude. My palate appreciates the flavors, and I chew every bite slowly. Now fulfilled with all the water I need for the rest of the day, I give thanks as I digest. The tip of the chemical balance meter is cold against my head, checking my levels. The reading states that I can go 22 more hours before I need to refuel again.

One little protein powder pill will do to handle my sugars. Learned that my body is a finely tuned vessel, and it responds to everything I do in my life. The key to keeping myself balanced is knowledge of self. I can still recall stories my Mother used to tell me each time I would break my chemical balance-

"Romas, why should you eat some much sweet food," she would say, "don't you have enough energy to run around today?"

"Dear Mother, this sweet candy was given to me by Sister Morals. I could not say no to her. She insisted that I have it, and I didn't want to be disrespectful." I explained to her, as I took another bite.

"Have a seat, my son. Let me tell you a story back when I was growing up." I knew that I was in for a long lecture, more than having story time. She grabbed me by my face and took a piece of cloth out of her pouch to clean me. My Mother then pulled a chair out from under a wooden table in the soup kitchen. As she sat down, she took a deep breath. She was a kindhearted sixty-year-old woman who had no problem keeping up with a seven-year-old foster child.

"Sit down my son. Let me explain to you what gratitude means. Do you know what that word is?" I shrugged my shoulders and threw back my head in the chair.

"I didn't think so, honey. Well, long ago, a little boy who was around your age at the time, who lived in the same village that I come from, back in Ayacucho. He reminds me a lot, as you do.

"I do forget his name, but that isn't important. Well, one day the village had some visitors who were merchants from another town far away. They made acquaintances with the Priest of the churches and stayed for two weeks.

"The merchants sold everything from bread, rice, corn, and even sweets to the whole village. In exchange for prayers, they would give the town discounts. We were all satisfied with this, and everyone blessed to have them.

"One day the little boy went into town to where the merchants exchanged their business. He did not speak much, and he would often sneak around-avoiding others. A businessperson by the name has Xavier witnessed the young boy hiding under a table, running away as he was spotted.

"Not being able to do much about this Xavier would spend the next week seeing this young boy exhibiting the same behavior. The merchant suspected the young child to be a thief and he had enough of it."

"Dear Mother, but I don't steal." I protested to her.

"Quiet now, and eat the rest of your sweets." I knew better than to interrupt her stories at this point. "Now let me continue?"

"Clouds and hurling winds came along in the middle of the second week. The usual crowd that came to the marketplace did not gather. Several of the merchants, including Xavier, had not sold a single dime all day. It was as if the whole village was a ghost town. As the gusty winds picked up, the merchants found themselves in the midst of a fast developing storm.

"This day happened to be one of the biggest storms Ayacucho had seen in decades. Before any warning, the merchants and all of their goods were plummeted by rains of heaven. Xavier and his fellow businessmen tried desperately to save what they could from Mother Nature's forces."

At this point, I was on the edge of my chair and had not even noticed that I had ruined my outfit by dropping my entire sweets. I know that Mother had seen this. I could tell by the voice expressions as her story progressed on. I looked down at my pants slowly, looked back up at Mother, embarrassed. She gave me the beautiful and loving smile that I have always loved to see. I bent my head down to my shirt and licked off what I could, hurrying back to hear what happens next.

"It is okay my son. I need to wash your clothes. Now I can use your help." She gives out a warm laugh and pats me on my head.

"Where was I? Oh, now let me tell you what happened next." At this point, I know that she may have been making up the story the whole time.

I did not care about that at all. My Mother always made me feel better with her incredible stories about life. This is how I became a responsible man.

My Mother goes on to say, "After effortless attempts to recover any of the goods from the relentless storm, all merchants fled for shelter, except Xavier. When he had all but given up, he turns back to see the young boy running away in the other direction.

"Visibly upset and at a loss, Xavier decides to follow the young boy to find out who he is. The little boy dashes through floods of water taking shelter every few yards. It is apparent to Xavier that the little boy is leading him away, for he could have easily escaped.

"The next fifth-teen minutes it seems as if the two are running around in circles, playing through the storm with their lives. Finally, Xavier catches up to the young boy who climbs up a small hill not too far away from where the merchant's shops were set up.

"The boy rushes inside a small cave alongside the hill and waves Xavier to come in. Soaking wet and out of breath, Xavier looks around intensely, pleased and finally covered from the devastating weather outside.

"After gathering himself, he sees the young boy come out from the shadows inside the cave. The young boy has a nervous look on his face and a wool bag in one hand. Apparently shaken, the young child opens his hand just as Xavier begins to ridicule him.

"Inside the boy's hand was several seeds which he had collected from all of the merchants who had visited the village. To Xavier's surprise, he had found a couple more bags inside of the cave, which contained all of the dealer's crops and seeds to reproduce the plants.

"Before Xavier had realized what happened, the young boy had run out of the cave, disappearing into the rainfall. The merchant rested in the cave for the entire night and was left in disbelief of what had occurred." By this time, my mouth opened wide, and I was still as a tree. Mother, on the other hand, was near the stove preparing soup and taking out a loaf of bread for us to eat. I did not even smell the bread baking, completely into the story, which she has carefully constructed.

"Do you know what has happened, Romas?" Mother asked, gently. "You see son; the young boy had saved all of the extra items he was given by everyone in the village over the two weeks."

"Really?" This was the first time I moved a muscle in ten minutes.

"The whole town knew that a storm was on the way, and yet no one told the merchants. Had the little boy told the dealers they may not have believed him anyway." She replied.

Realizing now, my Mother had made me a bowl of soup to eat and a place to sit at the table. I did not know how hungry I was until hearing her story, and I understood that the sweets were not going to satisfy me. At that time, I did not correlate gratitude with her story, but I did read her message.

"You see, Romas. You can accept the things others have given you with gratitude. You can also repay the gratitude by giving what you don't necessarily need to someone else who may need it." Mother sits down next to smiles and me.

Since that point on, I would learn to expect a story instead of a lecture or punishment from Mother. Now that I realize it, she has never truly disciplined me. Every day in my mind, I have vivid memories of her. She is the only woman that I had in my life. Destined to find her. My purpose and a crucial part of my mission to saving her.

Ending my mediation period of the day, I return to my alertus and review some old files. Feel that this is going to be a long night. A few hours later, and my mood sensitizer arranges the new hue of the room to a shadow gray. My mind intensifies seconds after the change and the red light above, across the ceiling changes to a dark purple. The alpha waves blend into a fundamental change to my delight. Venice music. It is time to study.

9

THE ALERTUS SOURCE OF POWER bases on magnetic energy and thought impulses or brain waves. The Global Council had designed the device only to be used to the most experienced applicants to become Monitors. The essential qualification becoming a Monitor is having a photographic and near perfect memory. I have both, and my reasons for becoming an agent hold more than one meaning.

Life is about putting together the pieces of your puzzle. Collecting the pieces on the outside and then working from within. There are many jobs inside the Global realm. For employment, The Council precisely bases on whom they select to employ. I had no way of getting the job that I have without corruptive means. The most traditional way to become a member of the council is inheriting through a bloodline.

Since I do not know my biological Father, I could not take that chance. My biological Mother, however, is far from the Nun who raised me. If they found out who is my real Mother, they would have burned my application. Therefore, the best and easiest way to get in was to do what I do best. Hack my way into the Global Council union. I can say that after running away from home as a young child, this is by far the most useful craft I have ever learned. It has gotten me this far.

The metallic oblique table in my study room has a code sequence, which I release. A little tone hums to a frequency that produces sound waves upwards. I carefully hold the Alertus steadily only several inches above the table, which hovers in midair. At least I can stay here at home and use the monitor device to observe what is going on.

An overwhelming feeling of guilt consumes me when it comes to Lon. He remains the focus. Pressing against my temples with my fingers, trying to recall what happened back in the last underground night. *Ugh!* Frustration.

"Let me first check back to the underground. I need to see what's happening now."

The night remains empty, and the streets are bare immediately after the Sirens. I focus my attention to the entrance of the underground noticing the Crows are few and still. Navigate my way through the door. My mind levitates to where I first met up with Lon. There is a sense of sadness around the common areas and the statue grove. Evidence and word of the rapture taken place last night have fallen upon the organization's members. It is, however, pleasing to see that each of the leaders from each cult and sect visit Aiko to give her their prayers. She is barely hanging on and seems to show signs of guilt as well.

No other monitors can view the activities of the underground as well as I can. The underground has sufficient technology that seeks out any Predeterminism devices planted with significant interference measures to block out satellites. The many times I have visited the underground gives me more access when using the Alertus.

Maybe there are answers from last night? Retracing the misfortune hours ago along the shadows and the dense atmosphere is dismal. Have not figured out how I have the ability to show many details after things took place than when they are happening live. I believe it has to do with my anxiety- how I become dazzled and almost sedated by the supernal lights.

Scenes from last night in the statue park notice something familiarly striking. The old woman who had addressed the crowd of people with her speech shows an eerie hue or glow surrounding her aura. I focus on her immensely as I review the Watchmen harassment. The Alertus suddenly becomes static monitoring, as I attempt to locate the old woman after Lon and I arrive. I cannot make her out of the crowd for some reason but came to the conclusion that this may be the same color hue I saw during the Rapture of Lon. I shake my head and lose the signal.

I do not want to believe something tells me the woman is not what she appears. Little is to know about the Angelic realm and the different class of Angels the domain possesses. One particular type known as an Isoclone, the Angels that can take any form they see, and previous clone images as well.

Back to present time, after losing the alertus signal from last night. *Let me monitor for clues going on in the underground, live.* My attention draws me to a pair of leaders from the sects S.I.N and Illume, who have assembled on the outskirts of Narian- by the forest. This seems unusual for the two to have met so far out from the underground.

"So is what I hear right," states the leader of S.I.N named Dag, 'do you believe that the rapture of Lon is a result of the rumors in their organization?'

The head of Illume, called Levi, sits next to an old tree. "And what rumors might they be, Dag?" Levi is part of an organization who liberates members of the underground, reforming them to faith-citizens.

"I didn't mean that in a wrong way." Dag clears his throat. Although the S.I.N operate in force, they compel to remaining focused. Many of the S.I.N have been victims of Raptures due to their volatile nature and thoughts.

"If you are speaking of child sacrifices then speak before you seek. Seek not the source of your interpretation. I love my fellow brother, Lon; he is of good nature." Levi states. I can see both the two men are yielding weapons and remain on high alert inside their *converspeer*. The meeting between these two top leaders is a conflict of interest.

A flock of ravens propels from inside a tree, startling the men. The clouds in which the birds fly into are thick and shadow their flight entrance. Both of the leaders have wingmen East and West, yards beyond auditory.

"Dag, I understand your perception. The new world is not alleviant of deception. The sacrifice of souls is inside of the text, and the will of men. Inside the will of spirits and demons. The truth is only a belief agreed upon through a length of time. And often the very nature of patience does truth helplessly bend." Levi stands and faces the other direction.

"Look. I didn't come here to listen to no wizard riddle. I know who Lon is." Dag throws his hands up. "We are just trying to find out why he was taken by that damn Angel or whatever the hell it is. You all kill me at Illume, with mumble rhyming jumble. We need not be afraid of what to say. If I ever came across this damn Angelic realm, I ain't be the one scared. You and your people want to help this worthless underground scum get back to the new world. Men like me are going after the real evil.

"No one around this shitty earth, or planet, or where ever the hell we may be, attempts to combat anything. We just sit around like lost little helpless sheep, while those who control us dominate our minds. First, the earth is flat, and then it is round, then flat again. And on the other side of it is the deception. The truth is the damn lie has become the truth!"

"I comply along with your thoughts, Dag." Walks back to his seat. "Please, continue."

"I told you before. What side are you on anyway? The Global Elite? The Angels? These so-called Gods? Our whole civilization's existence is under the impression that there is something out there, in the universe for us to find. Tell me this, Phineas Nigellus; what do you believe is going on? Because we believe in the search for the bad guys, catching them and bringing them to justice." Dag is shaking at this point and sweating heavily.

"The time will run regardless of who keeps track. We can only respond to what is the law, and we must not react." Levi reaches in his pocket and tosses Dag a cloth. "The answers may not be in scientism. So please forgive my explanation my brethren, Dag. As long as the observer is observing, then the reality created, condemnation based on limited perception often causes the debates."

"You know what Levi; I'm sick and tired… what the hell?" Dag leaps backward as a Raven has fallen, seared out of the sky. The two leaders lean forward to look down at the indistinct bird burning on fire. Before either can say a word, dozens of birds plummet the same. The sky above surrounding the two men, a pitch-black sphere centering.

Without making a sound, the two leaders retreat opposite ways within seconds. Winds bounce around the escape routes of the pair, circling small tornado gusts. I begin to read the patterns of the atmosphere rise increasingly. Crack. Rocks, branches, leaves and debris clutter between the men's leg as they reach both wingmen to flee.

10

FEAR CONTROLS EMOTIONS. The only other emotion besides fear- love. All other emotions come from one of the two. Too afraid to run? One mistake and you die. The difference between life and death is one miscalculation. Walking on different tracks of an upcoming train distracts you from the real danger. Hearing the roaring sound of the train horn that passes by your left, ignores the howl of the one coming right from behind. Smack. Bad decisions kill.

The fleeing men reach their own wingmen, opposite directions from each by this time. "Get the hell up, let's go!" Dag snatches his man off his rear. Shaken and looking back the wingman's fear distracts himself, losing three steps falling behind his leader.

"Practice makes perfect. We don't run these drills for nothing." Levi yells. The pair of he and his man manages through trees, constructing each step.

Heading away from the forest to the underground, they progress.

The groups spread apart, one group twice the pace of the other. The slower group full with mistakes. The difference is night and death. The scene fled from evil. Never seen birds fall from the sky. I would have run as well. Anyone would.

An arsenic color in the sky. I gaze into the alertus, seems like I smell fire. I turn to my wall inside my home displaying the full image of chaos. Convert the scene into a 360-degree panorama array. The sky cracks lightning. Winds starting downward spin up.

A twenty-foot circumference falling from above to the ground. The circle is alive, moving at a rapid rate. The outside edges of the circle are a beam of light waves consuming trees, boulders, and debris. Dag's path, soon to be compromised.

Lightning spirals inside of the circle. A piercing whistle combined with thunder. The color of the sphere is muddy and dark. Nontransparent inner. The villainous destruction this ring possesses is revealing. Carnage and havoc.

I believe this is another type of Angel not yet seen. You would think that these beings would just appear out of heaven. That is what we are to believe from movies and books. The spirits cannot just appear and disappear like some genie. The spirits in the new world have to obey the new laws, however.

But why?

The event that is taking place before my eyes on my device is a phenomenon. The shifting of space and time in a paradox. I have concluded that this supernatural being is after Dag or his wingman. *The spirits I have seen are supernatural beings.*

Within a few seconds, the circle flashes in and out, each time reappearing yards apart. Closer and closer. Once on the ground and the earth below consumed? Black ash and smoke left behind. Dag is a distance away from his man, who crashes down, yelling in fear. The wingman screams can produce no more sound. The coil sphere approaches, a split second away, dissipating clockwise and threatening baneful. The smoke and whirlwind of the field evaporate, hosting a benevolent figuration. The supernatural being is facing the wingman, who back is to my view. The outline of the being's likeness is blurred. Large garment drapes over unfitting, covering distinctive appearance. The garment unthreads into floating ash cloth, in flames.

"Oh no… no. Oh God, help!" The Watchman cringes on his ass crawling backward. This damn supernatural being or demon has an unhuman-like manifestation. Sparks of fireballs and flames fly across its frame. I notice the same glow or hue I have seen in the other beings, circling its hands. The creature's hands come together only inches apart. Light bluish static increases.

The light is a flamed blue color as from the lighters on earth. The demon movements are seldom and manacle as if I see images of a ghost or something that is not here. The beast flashes his image- lightning bolts in and out. *Jesus!*

The poor man's back is now stuck against a tree; pants tore with holes and Leafs. His head is in between his legs as he is about to kiss his ass goodbye. Out of desolation, he grabs his gun, shoots first, and then aims. The bullets bounce past the demon; one shot through. In an instance, the being's hands separate, growing this static field. The energy rips apart the flesh of the man, piece by piece like a piranha. He screams in agony and torment. I have to turn my head at the site. Horrified. This is no damn Angel. *Oh, My God!*

Either you become a captive placed in a rapture world, or you die. I know not why the demon has come down to do the work of the Gods to this man. He may have just been cast into a realm had he not retaliated. The wingman's flesh- no more. His bones lay dismantled, turned to dusk. His gun, a red chunk of steel. The tree that held his back and consumed the last breaths left to timber-blazed fragments.

Crash. Static and Lightning. The clockward sphere begins, reverting counter clockwise. The energy from what appears to be the demon's hands stretches outwards inside the circle. The powers network as the beast rises its arms to a V-shape above its frame. What I witnessed next is a perplexing revelation. This supernatural being flashes beams into the clouds with a grim fulmination. A blast throws me back onto my couch. All my acoustics become gray noise and my alertus malfunctions.

My pulse is racing as my hair trickles with sweat beads. I am at a loss for words gasping. I can only assume that the two leaders and the last wingman had not seen what just occurred. Fortunately, I can record the events in my memory. Hope that the device does not defect enough to repair. These supernatural beings have the capability to effect the mechanisms of the alertus magnetic pulse. Two devices lost in a couple of days. *Damn it to hell and back!*

The egg colored wall has a tint from the display. My red carpet makes static into my feet. I look over at my plants along the room. Without moisture as if not watered in weeks. I look across the chamber to all my electronics. Surged. *This is impossible.*

No time for me to lose focus. Slow deep breaths in and slow breaths out. I have many questions in my head. The hardest presence to face is a reality. This cannot be life, as we know it; someone captured, with a moment's notice of time? I do not have the luxury of putting all the pieces together now. The most important thing for me to do right now is write down as much as I can. The many details that I have seen. I cannot afford to have this revelation held hostage in memory.

Yes. "I have some cloud storage files I can over until I get my device repaired." That is a benefit of skillfully planting some monitor devices in the underground. Footage uploads in real time in the event the devices found and confiscated by the leaders.

My night just got longer!

11

A COUPLE OF HOURS to sleep before I have to report to work. Drinking coffee at this time seems out of the question. This is too much to take in for one day. Easing off my red Acupressure Mat, reprogramming mantras and vibrational pattern waves through its speakers.

The time is 2:20 am. A dull faced unfortunate experience that I am dealing with laying on my back, bringing my knees bent in the air. Having even did any decent stretches. My plush ball rotates in the air as I toss it up along with worried thoughts. Higher and higher, it reaches the ceiling- still confused.

No use crying over spilled milk. Everything happens for a reason. These clichés are a bunch of bullshit. I have seen too many people lose their lives for no reason whatsoever. Who comes into the world only to die senselessly? In some way, I do understand why we have to pray to the Gods and why we must not kill. Why is it a sin in religion to kill or even commit suicide? Having schizophrenic thoughts can kill. No one can control the thoughts in their mind. Our thoughts come from nowhere. Not even yogis, gurus or monks can monitor their thoughts. They just learn how to accept. Controlling breaths you take is the key. *What the hell do I know?*

I, on the other hand, have people I constantly worry about; my mom, Lon, and Aiko. The vulnerable one of them is safe, even though Aiko is under care; and notified when she comes to the underground. It is not safe for a pint size down there, guarded with her caregivers in the new world. I rather Aiko is locked inside with the family who is looking after her. The leaders of Lon's sect were able to find her a family of faith-citizens who stay away from danger and the horrible streets for her protection.

The couple who is looking after Aiko have no children of their own. They use to run a daycare center out of their home for many years before the wars. The husband and wife look after Aiko as if she was their child. I could not have asked a better couple to give her the emotional support and prayer that she needs to get through her struggles, being alone after losing her whole family. I have complete access to the monitor devices in that family's home at work. Monitors at the Council have access to all devices in the faith citizen's homes across the world. 'The Determined Agenda,' some call it. We at work call it 'Predetermined.'

There are nearly three thousand Monitor positions, all working around the clock watching over citizens. At least at our complex. It is our job to keep them predetermined and within the new world. This is the only way the Global Council can obey the laws the Gods has put for us to live by. It is what keeps our planet moving and without destruction.

"Pray to the Gods. Have faith in the new world Gods. If not then the earth will stop, and the Gods will release down the Angelic Realm to Rapture us all." Do I believe that? Sure. Yes, I am a police officer for the mind and subconscious savior for the many. *So how does it work? How does the Monitor save his fellow faith-citizen slave puppets?* Asking myself that, as I do far less keeping in my work than most. To manipulate the servers or not, that is my question. Seriously, I don't have time to care about anyone or anything else in this new world crap.

No. My mission basis not on what I can do to save every faith citizen. I am under my own direct purpose; to protect the people I care about in this wretched world. Why else would I be risking my life breaking into the Global Chain of Command posing as a believer?

My coworkers who believe in that crap do their job well. They are hard-wired and programmed to save humanity. They care. I do not. We all care in some way or another. I need to protect the ones that are my family more than anyone else is. I did find the job description instilling. Studying this position carefully and remembering back when I started working like it was yesterday. I was impressed on my first capture. It is a story that I could never forget. A man and his family on the brink of all a rapture. A household tore apart and unstable.

Hurray! My first week at my new council job. The monitor device for this particular family home had been ringing like a grandfather clock. The father in question could not take losing all but his wife and kids. The rest of his family, gone, dead or missing. His name was Manton. A fifty-five old accountant who went all but insane, having to commit himself to Rapture. He could not stop the suicidal dreams he was having throughout each day. I remember him trying everything from hypnosis, meditation, and even the black market products.

Manton had come to a point where he felt the attack on his family, was a spirited attack on him mentally ruining his functionality. He feared to kill his family and to commit his own death. Then decided one day to push the distress button. Manton came willingly to the Global chambers for Rapture, so he could protect his own family.

The Global Council did one thing right. See, you can go one of three ways to a rapture. The Monitor, which I happen to be, can detect your thoughts through Predeterminism and have arresting militants or bounty hunting at your door within minutes to save you from the demons. You can have demons come before we can get to you. It is your choice. The part you fear. What the council has implemented to save the faith citizens is a distress button on each household monitor device. You can press that to save yourself.

In two of the ways, you come to us, or we come to you. The last way, well, the demons come to you, and we do not know where you end up. So where does faith citizen go when we intervene? They come to the Council Island, placed into an induced coma and sent into another realm. Simple. No longer are they a threat to our new world. Case closed. Let us all go watch the News in peace now. Problem solved, right? Not exactly. No one can govern how long this coma will last. And I have seen more come in than have made it back to the new world as Reformers. That is what the Rapture 6 is birthed. The realm we send the citizens who commit themselves. The others undertook to the discretion of the Councilmen to whichever domains fit their offenses.

I had the luxury of taking in Mr. Manton my first week on the job. Now left in a coma, in another realm. His family, safe yet he lay at rest with thousands in a crystalline matrix state of mind. Nothingness does not sound too bad. There is a funny saying at work:

'To be determined or to be predetermined.'

We, Monitors often reexamined by the Council, sort of reprogrammed if you will. We never know when or what type of protocols, decorum, civility, or submissions ordered at any given time. The Global administration has abolished all hope for free will and replaced it with 'Predeterminism.' From a free-will world to a Determined world, and now a Predetermined new world. The only ones who continue to debate the theories of 'Free Will' vs. 'Determinism' are those in the underground. The same rebels who have questioned the governing agencies throughout our history, I assume. The thinkers, conspiracy theorist, and recluses who have challenged each Nation's decrees and power structure.

The Council's thirty-three rulings across the new world have replaced all Nations' national anthems, pledges of allegiances, homages, adulations, and veneration. The Council has superseded all faiths with the one true faith of the Gods for every citizen.

The first decree is enforced to be recited to the top leaders of the Council and any officers of the land to validate all who are faith citizen obeying the God's laws. You expected to know this by the time you can say full sentences. The Abbess in the underground had alluded to The Great Truth. Not many people understand what it truly is. We all know the order of society in civilized governments is acceptance of a free will. There is still so much more to learn.

However, I know that responsibility is a human invention. Why? It would be ineffective in a world where choices could not impose. If you do not obey the enforced laws of the land, they punish you.

Wake up and smell the enforcement.

Whatever I feel right now is making me nauseous. My carpet is stale, and my feet fell the course scratches. The ceiling produces sweat droplets during the past monitor. Strange to say the least. All of the discoveries and research over this weekend has me exhausted. I only have a couple of hours or so until I start my workweek. Not like, I even could make it to the bed. Speak the correct temperature to my cooling system, and I adjust the lighting as well. My thoughts linger on top of cushion as I close my eyes. My family and friends will consume my dreams for another night. At least I will not be sleeping in sorrow for long. I will be anxious to get back to the lab and continue my findings.

The best part of my days on the Island are the debates we have with one another. Usually, I sit back and observe. Most of the refuting go on during the lunch hours. People from all over the planet, working in different positions with contravening views. Most of the people I work with on the Island have no clue that they are being monitored with everything they say.

Algorithms and behaviors are recording for the use of the Global Council. Sometimes I like to manipulate the converspiring. I know that it is cruel, but they do not know they are tested and spied on. Not my problem- it is their issue.

The best part of my job is that I understand what lengths the Council will go through to maintain the ordinance of the compound and integrity of their institution. It is plain and straightforward to find out if you do a little research and thinking. The active citizens who work the Council on the Island undergo reprogramming weekly. Hacking into the logs on occasion, I have noticed certain conversation and positions of topic completely change after a heated debate, just hours after a reprogram protocol. But what do I know? Well, I know enough to place a dissolvable tab in an imploder that I take to work. That way I can get back to my original state minutes after I am under a mental transformation protocol.

Even staying to yourself at the Council is risky. Everything we do in the new world can put you at risk.

While hundreds, at one point, would plea placement in Rapture 6 to avoid the lower realms of death, the Council created the volunteer program to save the citizens from the Angelic Realm.

Before the invention of the program, faith-citizens would turn to the underground to seek out low-level laws to break; that would not send the worst Angels to come and Rapture them. *Crazy to think about it.* The good news now, the same program the Council has created, I am going to use to volunteer myself.

12

THERE ARE DAYS when you have a lot on your mind, and it seems like your thoughts slip away from you, when you try to concentrate. My life is like losing my place in a book that I am reading. The only people who truly know me lived in my childhood. I never knew my dad, regret to think about my biological Mother. On the way to work, I left my anxiety pills at home again. My fears happen when I think about her, back then. Mother,

Traveling to work is more than an adventure; it is a quest. Painful and long. I know it is worth all that I am going through. Flying over 10,465 miles to work is common in the new world. Taking a supersonic train through the mountainous Antarctica, that is the exciting part. It is no roller coaster ride at a theme park. No one knows for sure how long the trip takes once we land on the Island to get to the Global Council Complex-a-thon. The trip will take up to a day for me one way, so I schedule to stay on the Island my entire work week. My job will begin on this damn plane for the next shift, however, and by the time I get to work a full two days will have passed with the time difference. Another reason why I hate to do work at all when I arrive at my station. *The Joy.*

Some 15 hours or so later, I arrive to land on the Island. The complex is in the middle of nowhere. Some say that the Gods rekindled the complex into existence. If this is true, then the heavens must still be on our side. *Offer up faith prayers to the Gods who have rekindled the world.* Being here brings out the best in me, sarcastically speaking. Others say that the compound was in first developments, back in the early 1900's. In any event, The Global Superior have kept the poles off the map for over a century. *Why was there a treaty not exploring Antarctica you say?* Far as I know, we are not anywhere near Antarctica. Deception rules the sheep and controls the week. *Poetic.*

We arrive at a vacuum train, which does not move unless it has the correct weight of each individual with secret security clearance, onboard. I have a perfect memory for profiling each passenger, which comes in handy when I bypass the system, to cover my absences. I would like to take credit for the McKinnon virus I uploaded at my employer's facility, the problem is, and I hacked the virus from someone. A computer genius I am not; people tell me, too smart for that. The truth is I am a smart ass to the people here, and I have no friends that even speak to me. Not here for these people. If they knew who I am, they would process me directly into Rapture Zell.

The same elderly woman holds the door open for me as if this was a subway. I tell her that she does not have to keep the door; it is all programmed and sophisticated. She just replies, "Heh?" She reminds me of an old Gypsy woman I met when I abandoned the church. That is somewhat mean to say. However, I always felt that the Gypsy woman could tell I was a thief and a con artist, already at the age of 12. She may have even known that I had a foster Mother because she would mention, "Sweet Sister Romas."

The train has a perfect weight, and the doors all close concurrently. There is no need to sit unless you want to. The Global Council has an absolute importance for details. Nothing happens here by mistake. Before every trip on this train, the voice on the intercom noticeably clarifies:

[Ding]

'Greetings citizens of the new world. You have arrived by flight 48465a at 0400, to Latady Island, Antarctica. You are aboard underground train Yetti 510a. Your destination coordinates 70°45'S 74°35'W. Your travel time may vary for security reasons or concerns. Thank you. Enjoy, and remember, have unconscious, content thoughts.'

It always kills me to hear the same announcement each morning. The crazy thing is, if you do not pass the security scan to get on the plane and on the train, Official escort off, into the processing center. That is what I did a few months ago, with the help of some prosthetics so no one would view my beautiful features. Breaking out of the processing center was easy. However, not as fun as getting my position to work here, right after escaping. Well, maybe installing my virus over the next few days, took the cake. The credit goes to the streets.

You can never see the outside of this supersonic vactrain. You sure and the hell ain't see it go by at 1,200 mph. The room that opens the doors to go inside the train is the only thing you see. I prefer to stand strapped up, while some others choose to sit. The process does not take long. The only thing I hate is the three minutes before we take off. Across the top inside of the train is a digital text strip. You know what time the train will be leaving when this red strip lights up, counting down from 2:59. Faith citizens call these last three minutes before we leave, the Converspeer period. Right on cue, the voice on the intercom goes into full detail and explains:

[Ding]

'You may now begin, Converspiring. Converspeer is to speak from within to others as a form of communication routed from the soul. One of the goals is to create a form of communicating that will bypass normal conversing, to having men connect subconsciously. Your three minutes start, now.'

I hate this part. Struggling to secure the last strap on a leg is a tall man with a beard from a barbershop quartet. He stands to my right side every morning to have our little, *'Talk.'* He catches his finger in the straps. "Whew. Already at 2:46 and counting." He laughs out, trying apparently to play it off. "Maybe I should start over with a Mantra?"

"Just stop talking to me." I look away.

"But, we are converspiring, my beautiful friend." He replies. "Breathe in, om. Breathe out, om. Most women are braver than most men are. A female who is physical with a man that is not hers is like a train, it takes a lot to start it and a hell of a lot to try to stop. Love is energy. Fall in love with someone who deserves your heart, not someone who plays with it. When you know exactly what it is you desire you don't accept anything less or keep anything other.'"

"Yeah, touché. We have 2 minutes left. Are you finished now?" I would give anything for this train to start moving and to get this heart-to-heart over. At least, when we do start and reach max speed, no one can hear you speak, so no one does. I should not be rude to the barbershop quartet guy. I understand the importance of converspiring for the faith citizens. One of the forms of communication and speech, section groups along with the Global Council, deemed protected. People in the new world do many different things to avoid, Predeterminism and especially, the Angel realm. "Well, I rather see you doing something positive to stay in the new world, instead of going out into the streets and using alternative devoirs." I turn my head back away.

The new world is with demonic spiritual transformations, sacrifices, and criminals. The black market overflows with new technology designed to help you deter from thoughts of killing a person. Many people create vices that are bogus and ineffective. The Predeterminism system implements to stop you before you kill someone. The last thing the earth needs is the

Angels coming to collect more souls to send to the Rapture worlds. At least that is the last thing a citizen would want.

"39 seconds more. Please, reach out to me and speak from your soul." The giant man is persistent at best. He always finds a way to converse with me. Now that I think about it, he would be the one who would know if I did not show up to work. Him and the gypsy woman. Don't see this turning out well for me. I lift my head and close one eye.

"Love, and value yourself. You are God's creation, and He paid a dear price for you to be alive today." He looks at me and turns away with his mustache crooked. When you converspeer, it has to be from within. People in the new world often speak in riddles and rhyme to stay focused.

I smirk and look back at him. "If you aim at nothing, you'll hit it every time." The man may not have an appreciation for my witty charm. *What do I care?*

The red timer fades away as the 2:59 minutes are over. A subtle pressure builds up around the enclosed compartment of the train. I close my eyes; imagine a mixture between a baritone and a French horn as the train low frequencies hum. Finally, we depart.

13

HIGH PITCH TONES pop my ears notifying me that we have arrived at our final destination. I heard of employees mistakenly on the far side of the mountain by accidentally boarding the wrong vacuum train. No one knows how much of the 1,300 square mile island the council has developed, or if it is a transition. I would not want to be lost in Antarctica, inside one of the unknown territories myself. After all, this is not Area 51.

I read inside my hologram email I display along the corridors, the new security procedures for our facility. A hologram email designs to alert the recipient of critical confidential documents, wherever they are located. Personally, I think that having a hologram email is a waste of technology when the lighting to view it needs to be perfect under specs. Expertise in the new world is far from common sense. The employees of this sophisticated, Complex move in an orderly fashion, well aware of the rules and regulations, which methodically prompts:

[Ding]

'Welcome to the Global Council Predeterminism Authoritarian Facilitation. Please dispose of any new world technologies that are ungoverned before entering your stations. If you witness any anomalies or anything unusual, please contact the proper authorities. Please think highly of others and remain legally determine. Thank you for being a giving faith-citizen.'

The new world programs with updated announcements that circulate through every single communication stream on the earth. I like to joke about these updates by referencing to them as the new amber alerts our society we received some 30 years ago. The truth of it is that these updates frequently follows someone deposited into a Rapture for defying the Gods laws. No one would have thought abduction by an Angel a few decades ago was a terrifying experience. Welcome to the year 2052.

Processing takes over an hour to arrive at my station and begin my next shift. I deputized a coworker of mine when I realized he had invented a tendency program to simulate daily tasks, which concludes how much work achieved based on the current mood of the worker.

I have to tell him that his invention is good, even though I hacked into it and never actually do any work here.

I am not a hacker; it is enjoyable to locate the information I need. Nor am I a thief taking what is necessary, so I do not have to wait to possess it is convenient. The truth is I have been a thief since a runaway and a horrible liar. The lab doors behind me open up, and a young man enters inside of the workstation to my area. As he approaches me, I close the tendency simulation I have hacked, before the inventor's knowledge,

"Romas, hurry. You're going to miss transport." He runs past me, knocking over a chair. Falling to his knees bumping his head on a desk. He places his tie on his head making a bloody mark and then runs around to reach his computer station "I'm fine, I'm fine.

Let me pull up the transport log on my workstation. Take a look at what I found."

"Where is the fire?" My feet fall from the desk. "Can't you see I'm not working here?" I follow him to his workstation and pretend to portray an interest to this revelation, disregarding his ineptitude. I call him Lufton. His parents are right wing Republicans who converted to Democrats, after the 2020 elections. There is a few reason why his revelation is not a surprise at all, however.

'In the new world, everything happens for a reason. Our world is created, and we are faith-citizen offering up our beliefs to the Gods.' The computer screen states the beginning of a new world 'Pledge of Decrees,' when Lufton logs on. A nuke bomb one a red, white and blue new world flag displays on the monitor. I have to admit that this was my doing. After a 45 second clip of an Angelic takeover reenactment, he finally opens up a classified area in the system. Sweat begins to fall down Lufton head across from his bruise.

He turns up his chin, "Excellent, right?" His teeth show from ear to ear. "Did you think that you were the only one with superb hacking skills?"

My eyes cut directly down, "You do look a bit brighter since you took that fall." I realize he knows that I am the one who hacks into his profile. "So what is the big uproar about?" Staying calm, I have a few days before he realizes that I also gave him access to these logs. Everything happens for a reason. I run through my head. The unit that Lufton and I assign to is Predeterminism surveillance sector 2031. The council created this group to oversee the satellites, earth cams, and independent deters monitors in each household in the Island's regions.

"I noticed some strange citizen activity when reporting individual law violators. When my alarms came on for the latest offenders, it wasn't because of Predeterminism." He points to three citizens on his screen.

"Ok, speak less like Sherlock and more like a conspiracy theorist, would you?" I scratch the itch on the tip of my nose.

"Ok, well usually I get an indication of my system, I can tell soon as citizens thoughts to kill someone happens, as in all of ours right?" His hand drops from the screen and opens up. "The last three residents here all committed to being brought in, yet their vital signs register as showing them shocked to be escorted here by the authorities."

"Maybe they wanted to take a hot shower and get some sleep before they were put to rest." I nod my head and step back. Lufton does not seem too thrilled for my distance. I need him to piece together the puzzle before anyone else finds out I am breaking the law. "So what are you getting at, exactly? I still have to pretend like I'm working you know."

His hands come together, "So, it seems to me as if the three citizens did not want to be put to sleep and commit to going to a Rapture realm. I would rather be placed in a machine then cast away by a demon Angel, but what if they didn't want either?"

"So you are saying that they were pure faith-citizen offering prayer to the Gods, and we took them in without justification?" I take a deep breath and exhale.

"I didn't, but you did." He winks and grabs his bruise as we laugh. Haven't shared a genuine laugh since I last seen my Mother at the church I grew up in. I have not been close to anyone since I was a child. Every person I am involved with is for a reason. It is never by chance. You seldom find the right answer by relying on chance.

I cannot say if he has received enough information at this point. Tapping his shoulder, I head to the desk with one eye open. "So, I still need to know how good I feel about completing my tasks for the rest of the day."

"Amusing, Mr. Computer illiterate." He places his feet on top of his desk as his chair squeaks. The ground trembles as I return to my section and the doors are automatically open to our station. Gaze back at Lufton realizing that only deter Monitors as ourselves can open up the doors to our section. Turn back to the view the door opened midway and notice several co-workers dart down the hallway past us. Lufton falls out of his chair and still manages to beat me to the door. The entrance is made of windows that display new broadcasts and protocols. With a code, the windows turn back transparent to an entire warehouse filled with transportation vehicles to maneuver around the compound.

"Hey, where are you guys going? Wait for me." He springs down the hallway behind the group. Return to my desk to access my program, uninterested. I enable my virus to upload a breach protocol that I have created using this commotion. The virus is a program to start the first phase as soon as we unlocked Lufton computer, by causing a vehicle in the compound below us to create an accident, allowing a few faith- citizens to escape it the process. I carefully reroute all of the technical deter equipment in the station to bypass, allowing me a few minutes to go undetected.

My co-workers reach the end of the corridor to find several citizens in a mini civil war with security, down in the vehicle hanger. Every other few seconds I hear bursts of laughter at the entertainment, they are enthusiastic to view, giving me my sense of how much time I have. The doors to the station remain open as a cool breeze flows through the hallway. I can hear a couple of doors open and then close with footsteps that follow coming in my direction. I slowly turn around to see a man with long white hair and a dreaded beard, leaning in the door opening. The footsteps belong to an underground citizen who belongs to the anonymous group. His name is Cane.

The steps that the man cautions are of my invited guest. Easing his temperament, I lift my right hand to show him my palm as he enters. Cane is a leader in the movement that went against the new world order for decades before the wars. He is one of the last high leaders we know of. This man has been searching for the other leaders for a long time. Cane's mission has become as mine; searching for lost friends, family, and answers about the diabolical Raptures.

14

CANE STEPS CLOSER and looks across the top of the room.

"Are you the lone one that we seek to establish? The shadows amend laws we seek being abolished."

"You don't have to worry. I turned off the machine, so we have a few minutes to converspeer."

"Let me make this quick. There is a belief that we have where I come from. Many decades ago, the old world divided and controlled by what we would consider evil. In the midst of this evil, humanity held a single note of faith. The Elite used division, colonialism, created racism to conquer and generated wealth to control. Yet, nothing was a most potent weapon they possessed until they were able to determine the world's faith in God." His throat clears. He slumps down into a chair and breathes in deeply.

"Please continue Sir." This has been a long journey for Cane, and I successfully made it possible.

"If you are trying to find a reason, do not bother. If you want to find a solution, you are wasting your time. If you have suffered beyond disbelief, then you are among the many. There will be nothing you can do overthrowing belief. As long as the elite have this, the elite will have us." Cane's cough startles me. "It is time for me to reach our other brothers in the Rapture. I pray you will do your part as meant. Nothing is by accident. Everything IS, for a reason."

"I will do what I can to make your deposit into the Rapture, less painful. You better follow the program and get back to the hanger." The last time I gave someone my complete attention was Mother, back in Cuenca. Even though it will only be a matter of time for the authorities at the Council to learn about the breach I have made, I am successful at obtaining the necessary piece to move to the next stage in my mission. The dark thoughts about my Mother well-being are constant, and I can only hope that she is somewhere here in the new world and not lost in Rapture Zell.

Time to close down the program and restore the Deter system in the station. When I turn around to look, he is gone. Correctly timed as the authorities finally assemble the remaining citizens who I help led to escape briefly. Laughter echoes down the corridor, and I see the crew from the nearby station pass by our doors. Lufton stands with one foot in the room and one foot out, laughing as he reenacts one of the prisoners ruffed up. He heads tilts back at the ceiling, and the deter system reads his chemistry assuring me that I successfully restored it correctly.

"What happened? Did I miss you bust your ass again?" I wipe my face with a half-smile.

"Ha-ha, funny. Where were you at?" He sips a cup of water on his desk. "I don't care; I changed my password anyway."

My head falls forward into my lap. I haven't laughed this hard in years. Those few minutes of fun warrants a deep breath as I go into deep thought and begin to meditate. I think that destiny does somehow put people, things, and sometimes places together. I can always find a person that I had in my life who changed it in some way. It is like when two people cannot remember something in particular unless they try to do it together. The world will not move on given these two individuals if they do not reach a rational conclusion to the imposed dilemma.

Time does not move for a moment and then many even hold their breath for a few seconds, during union in thoughts. No two people can share this alike. This is why we hold on to the spiritual things. It is when someone has control over our spirits that we are lost. The good news is that power does not mean ownership. You can only give up ownership over something you create, and no one is the Creator but the Creator.

There are plenty of good people still left in the new world, most of whom work in the compound on this island, along with some members of the Council Elite. This is a real good job with no incentives or pay. There is no longer wages or Governments, as we know of.

There are no countries stronger than the other is. We are all faith citizens in the controllable unified organism.

The next two hours of our shift go by as usual. I can forget that I did not bring my pills with me to work, and it is all thanks to the unfolding of the day at work so far. The top of the ceiling illuminates giving the indication that we have an update to our station.

"You have been quiet about that thing that happened earlier." He turns his chair and leans backward.

"Exactly. There is nothing unique or different about today from any other day. Everything happened the way it was supposed to happen." I reply. I change my attention to my screen. Sitting forward, he turns to face me. He takes a sip of his hologram cup, which shows the contents inside.

"Well, since you put it that way, let me ask you a question? You say everything happened today the way it was supposed to happen. What about in another realm?" He asks.

I drop my head on my desk to make a light blow. "What are you talking about now? Should I explain it in a Ted Talk or an old fashion Trump tweet?"

"We all know about the Rapture realms, which clearly states different dimensions. We work in a facility to place the citizen in a trance sleep and simulates other realms. So how can all of these various planes co-exist? Not to mention the Angelic and God Realms." His voice almost raises another octave.

This is what I have been waiting for. To be honest, I had to program a sequence of past announcements and play some theta waves under the music in the station. I feel as if I am running out of time. Lufton is the only insider I have to work with. I have to let him believe that it is his own conclusions he finds to allow him to board. "Whatever you are saying, what are you trying to get at?" Itch the side of my head with interest.

"I'm saying before the wars took place, the old war was under the control of the New World Order. We now live in a new world. In both the new world and New

World Order, we are doing the same thing. Believing in something new." He looks up and to the right.

"Well, I see that you are trying to figure out something. I am just here. Now please, be quiet." I bang my head on the desk again. He is on the right track. I pick my head to address where I need this converspiring to go. We simultaneously turn towards the door noticing a different person entering besides any of our co-workers. We look to see three authorities come into our station. Two younger men, grand in stature, follow the man who is in charge. The Captain of the trio is a Councilman, named Sen. Davis.

"As you were gentlemen. As you know, we had a security breach not too long ago near your section, and I wanted to stop by to ask you two a few questions." Sen. Davis approaches us with his shoulders broaden. "You both have failed to send a report as to what you witnessed happened earlier in the hanger below you, and as you know, sending a report is part of the protocol."

"Good afternoon, Sen. Davis. I was under the impression that it was to be completed today." I stand up and focus. "I was not made aware of a timeline."

"You were under something, alright! If that happens again, you will be under suspicion. We also noticed several computer spikes from your section. What could you tell me about that?" Sen. Davis's focus turns directly to me.

"I didn't know my hologram cup was listed as a new world technology item as of 1159 Sir." Lufton raises his see through cup. "So when I came down the hallway with it to witness the breach, it may have gotten scanned by the system. I briefly had to shut it off so that the authorities didn't think we had a violation on our level." Sen Davis and I open both our eyes wide with amazement at what just happened.

"That didn't make any God damn sense." Sen Davis replies. "I will be sending a unit to do a sweep of your log and an investigation." He turns without making any eye contact and makes a pass straight down the corridors. I flopped down in my chair as the wingman sighs aloud. Faced red with embarrassment, we realized that Lufton covered our asses most ridiculously. His tie dabs the mark on his head. It must still hurt when he smiles. I, on the other hand, know that I am running out of time.

15

LUFTON SHOWS NOTHING but his teeth. "You can thank me later, Sherlock." He says, sitting back on his desk with a smile I have gotten used to since I started my shift. I start to feel as if he is holding back on me and knows more than he is willing to admit at this point. Both of our monitors send out a vibrant shake, which makes my partner fall back losing his feet from under him. The top of the building flashes briefly, and the walls of the building begin to buffer. An announcement usually posts at the same times. The voice of the report begins:

'Attention sectors 2012 -2031 of the Deter monitored units. We have a new protocol implementation to enforce immediately following this announcement. Please do not disconnect, log off your computers, or leave your stations for the next 2 hours. Your cooperation is actively enforced and muchly appreciated. This has been a Global Council approved certified message.'

Slump down in my chair. I glaze over at Lufton who immediately does the same. I realize that I have been at work longer than anticipated, and I may have to orchestrate the next phase sooner than expected. However, it will draw too much attention to me unless I have Lufton involved in my plans. The screen flashes on my monitor and each other display in the station follows. The light at the top of the ceiling point inwards to shine onto each other leaving behind several red lights, which circle beneath. We both jump out of our chairs and rush to the projector at the far side of the room which has not been on all day. The tint of the chamber lower and a slight buzzer sounds to indicate the doors are locking. This is the last thing that I need. To be trapped inside of the station.

There is an old saying that states, 'At the end of a rainy day there is always a shining rainbow.' For Lufton, this rainbow has a big pot of gold at the end, and for me, I am more interested in defeating the Leprechaun who is guarding the pot. Lufton has never been in the station when the unit is under security protocol. He has just made it to becoming a full-time monitor the last few weeks.

"I can't believe this is happening right now." With his palms on the main desk, Lufton lifts himself up to get a better view.

"Move out of the way. We are the only ones here." I grab him down to calm his excitement. This will be both of our first times to see a Rapture inside the Global Complex. I have not been working in this position long enough to monitor an Angel come to claim a citizen with all of the station's technologies. Some of the citizens in the new world never even confined to the faith given to the Gods. Other residents stay underground like the few that are under the leadership of Cane. Still, many people who commit crimes including murder that even Predeterminism cannot stop. When this happens, the Angels come, and that soul who committed the crime could descend straight into Rapture Zell for eternity.

Lufton snaps his fingers, cracks his knuckles, and taps his feet all at once. "I read about the Angels while studying to become a monitor. I wonder what kind of Angel is coming to the new world to capture this poor guy. Ha-ha?"

"Will you stay focused?" I snatch him down pulling him behind me. When this spirit enters our world, I need to take mental notes as well as the readings. We have the documentation of all the Angels, but when it comes to the God realms, we could see any type of spirits transform out of the heaven.

The good thing about being in the station is that we can view the Raptures with the help of our satellites almost in real times if the spirits so happen to allow us. If you were there in the world when a Rapture happens you have a rare chance to see it first hand, and it really is not what anyone would wish on his or her worst enemy. There is a long enough warning that we have when a Rapture is about to take place. Many people often wonder how we can see this phenomenon at all. Some think done purposely by only Angels to evoke fear and compliance.

"I read that we will get a reading before the Angel appears out of the heavens, yet we still will not know where it's exact parameters will be until the precise moment it arrives," Lufton explains. "I know I sound like I'm reading out of a book. Hey, Romas, I remember the time you said you witnessed a Rapture. Come on; I have to ask about it? This will be a perfect time."

I did not know what to think when he asked me this. I had never gone into full detail about my experience first-hand with an Angel. A few people know that this happened to me, and for that matter, there are very few people here to tell about it. The fact of the matter is that I have seen multiple Raptures.

Lean back on the desk behind me. I glance up at the middle of the ceiling. Imagine the lights as bright as the ones I witnessed a few years back. Figured since I am almost out of time I may as well connect with the only person who can help me through this. Take a deep breath. Look down to the floor. My hands are on the top of my head, and I walk several steps away.

Lufton eyes are twice as big as I have seen them before when I turn around.

Time was running out for me. I need to access my program to send Cane to the correct Rapture. I need to implement my exit strategy, and now I feel compelled to make sure that my co-worker is safe through the whole thing. Backing towards him, I begin to explain. "As you know I didn't always have it easy growing up. I found myself lost most of my life, having to swindle my way around. I was a man by the age of thirteen. I had the ability to manipulate my way through whatever obstacles that were in front of me.

"I found myself alone and didn't trust anyone. After the wars had ceased and the New World Order failed to produce Global domination, I had a chance to join the Global Council. I decided against it. Then after they developed the Predeterminism technology, I followed the rules to stay in this world and vowed to find my mother one day so that she would never have to witness the wrath of these Angels." I continue as his eyes and mouth are the same lengths.

"I found myself looking for some answers in the underground shopping through the black market. Not to use any of the comic creations, but to see why so many people were against the Council. We had just been through war after war. We had been countries at the end of extinction. And then out of nowhere comes to these creatures telling us to give faith to some Gods."

I turn to look at the projector screen and read the levels of the transitioning. I have to make sure that I do not miss any other readings or distinctions, so I turn to the side not to take my eyes off the screen and continue.

"I met a few shady characters in those times. The one who this story is about, his name is Octavier. He was a ruthless man and had the street smarts to make any school professor change his curriculum the next day after they met. However, before Predeterminism, he was a career criminal. He witnessed his only sister die in the wars, and after that had changed his life; he was determined to go after the

Elite society, singling them out for the rebellion." I glanced back over to Lufton to make sure I have not put him to sleep. I know his type, and he seems to be waiting for me to get to the action.

"Well, Octavier could not go back to his gang because they were in the killings, and he couldn't go join any of the underground movement. Therefore, he would gather lone wolves like me and run around the city to cities trying to bring down the Elite. He approaches a high profile banker in the sapphire district who had lost everything and was hooked on drugs."

"'Look at who I found Tate. Mr. Fisher Price himself.'"

"I turn around to see Octavier holding a grown man off the ground."

"Wait, who is Tate again?" Lufton interrupts.

"I am Tate. Well, that is my first name. At least that is the nickname I was given by the church." I take a glance back at the screen and notice some conducive energy building around region 9. I calculate anywhere from 5-15 minutes before we get any evidence. The amount of the Angels that are coming to Rapture has increased substantially in the last week. It is uncommon for a rekindling of the Gods to happen without detection or cause. To my knowledge, people at a Compound Facility Complexes across the new world glued to the monitors awaiting the Global Councils announcements.

16

CONTINUING WITH MY STORY as I start to feel some anxiety build up. I keep the screen in the corner of my eye and stare directly at Lufton. "Look, let me just get right to the point. You don't want to be around these Angels. Octavier saw enough of the Angels Rapture innocent people. He perfected himself to be a master mind-stalk."

"You have to be kidding me." A smile comes over Lufton face. "You were able to be around a mind-stalk, and you didn't become a captive? How on earth did you do that?"

"I told you I was a master con-artist. I always had something to give, so I was too valuable to lose." My head pounds more each time an interruption. "You are right, most people who hang around mind-stalks ultimately fall victim to the mental traps and often think about killing themselves. That is the reason why mind-stalks can get away, and leave the victim to his own thoughts. Next thing you know, it is too late. In comes a demon while the criminal is long gone.

"Let's just say that I had no idea Octavier would want to witness an actual demon cast a soul. It was a bad time to stay and watch. Some of the Angels don't care for individual men at all and only kill the citizens." My eyes fixed on the system readings.

"Are you saying that you walked into an actual killing?" Lufton jumps off the table. He does not land entirely on his feet and falls onto the floor again. We realize that the level of the lights above us starts bouncing from off the wall. I turn to view the projector to see that there are no signs of any new activity.

"Change the reading to thermal view." I direct to Lufton. "Turn on the seismology readings." My voice begins to tremble dropping to a lower octave. All of the lights inside our station flash off. The only light inside the room is old floodlights. A howling Siren blasts through the intercom and the doors remain locked.

"Oh no. Is this the real thing?" Lufton shouts under a desk, he falls. Trying my best to get him to stay calm, but there isn't any use. The main projector detaches from the beams and slams onto the ground in front of us. Whack. Glass and sparks fly everywhere. By this time, I am looking for the emergency exits as my co-worker screams like a church girl. We hear several cries down the corridor as the doors pry apart. With a

Crowbar in one hand and a flashlight in the other, I witness Sen. Davis standing in the doorway with his sleeve cover in blood.

"Get the hell up. Hurry up. Go. Go. Go!" Sen Davis swings his bloody arm to indicate the coast is clear. "I'm still sending in for that investigation on your asses. Get the hell out of here."

"What? Wait, what are you doing Sir?" I jump up and drag Lufton by his pant leg across the doorway. "Sir?" Soon as we reach the exit, Sen Davis darts into our station dodging debris falling inches away. He turns around to me and tosses the flashlight in my direction.

"I still need to sweep your logs. How do I know you don't cause this earthquake?" Screaming at the top of his lungs, Sen. Davis trapped between us, and an array of ceiling panels.

"Is his ass crazy?" I fall into the halfway as Lufton pulls me away. "What the hell are you trying to do Romas? Come on before you end up dead like that lunatic in there."

I fall to the ground and try to look past the smoke inside to locate Sen. Davis. I am not worried about saving his life. The codes to get to the correct Rapture simulation sequence are at my desk now on top of Sen Davis and underneath the entire ceiling. Considering an early grave, I view down the hall to see that I have another problem ahead of me. Lufton is holding onto a beam suspended downwards into the hanger, after jumping through a broken window in the passage.

"Oh no. Oh, my God. Tate. Tate!" I can barely hear Lufton screams in between the chaos of people fleeing the area.

Finally, lift up to my feet and notice a man has picked me up off the ground. This man is much larger than I am and pulls me toward his direction. I dig my feet into the ground of the hallway and try to release to head back to safe my friend. Cannot manage to escape the powerful grip of this man, and I turn my head down the hallway to discover Lufton. The corridor filled with smoke by this point, and I suddenly feel another pull on my shoulder.

"Romas, Romas. Hey man, what's wrong with you." Lufton looks at him and shakes his head. "You have been standing here with that weird look on your face for 5 minutes." Gasping while swallowing some saliva, only to realize I had been in a broad day vision. To my pleasure, I look around to find that we are still in the station, and everything is still in place. Putting both of my hands on Lufton, I smile. Turn around and look at my desk behind me. A small notepad on the edge of my desk I extend to grab and place in my lab coat.

"Are you okay man. What is with the notepad? We supposed to be are all electronic." Lufton seems more confused at this point.

"Let's just say that; you never know when you are going to need to have something to write with until it's too late." Retake a deep breath and turn back to the projector screen. "Oh, and can you keep the seismology monitor up?"

The next ten minutes go by, and my co-worker, nor I say a word. His eyes glued to the projector. I, on the other hand, am much more proactive and start to input the codes for the Rapture simulation. I am glad that my co-worker has not pressed on the issue about the Angel story. I believe that thinking about the past has stirred up my anxiety and cause me to have that dream.

More tasks take importance. Besides, if Lufton gets lucky, he may soon witness what he is looking for. As for me, I have to make sure I export the correct coordinates for Cane. If I make a miscalculation, he could end up in an infinite state, or worst, I could mistakenly send him to Rapture Zell. Something tells me that Octavier ended up in Zell. It all depends on the demon who cast you away to whatever Rapture they choose based on the law violations you committed.

I am done with Cane's coordinates. I have a few more minutes to reprogram the contact details of the other violators. Lufton was indeed onto some things he implemented earlier. A few of the other citizens who came in with Cane were never violators of Predeterminism, nor did they want to commit themselves. For me to continue to stay inside the compound undetected, I had to program my McKinnon virus to act as the real citizen who here, were the ones hacking the complex from the outside. Everything happens for a reason. The citizens were hand selected and vetted by me to join Cane in the Rapture realm. None of these men would have volunteered to go and invade the simulation the Global Council initiates. No one would have gone into the Rapture that I know of except Cane and myself.

I finish the last sequence and start to format my entire log from the first day I got here. That dream about Sen. Davis left a mark on me. Check to see if the security has released the lock on the doors to our station to no such luck. Convince my co-worker to unite with override and me the locks may have to happen. *Just great.*

"Have you noticed any new activity, Sir?" I ask politely.

"Sir? What the hell got into you, Romas? Sen. Davis?" My co-worker sips some coffee and laughs.

"Never-mind. So tell me, what else do you do on your workstation beside spy on women through your, deter monitor?" I grin back to him.

"So I guess you do spy on me, son of a bitch." He takes a swing at me. I catch his arm in the air and place him in a lock.

"Now you do know that my Mom was a nun right?" I release his arm, and we both let out a loud laugh. "But, no. I didn't know you were a perv. I was just practicing some mind-stalk techniques on you." I haven't had this many jokes in a long time. Still, cannot hold on to the joy for long, as it is short-lived. I keep the sincerity of our situation the focus of why I am here.

A second tone resonates across the intercom that we have not heard before. The voice on the intercom proceeds:

[Ding]

'Thank you for your faith. We here at the G.C.P.A.F have implemented the following protocols as follows. The year of 2057, the month of JULY, the day of estimate 3rd, execute the following new laws to be determined as Predeterminism. Please, do not record, or write down the following statutes, for it is unlawful and will result in severe Global punishment.

New world action laws:

1. No faith-citizen is to be determined during the estimated day of Sun-times 2359 to 0159 unless instructed by a high official in the Council Elite.

2. No deter monitor technology is to be implemented during the expected day of Sun-times 2359 to 0159 unless notified by a top official in the Council Elite.

3. No member of the organizations outside of the faith citizens shall be determined by the estimated day of Sun-times 2359 to 0159 unless instructed by a high official in the Council Elite.

'These new laws will be imposed with direct oversight from the Gods in the next resolution to the Angelic realm within the seasonal offerings. Again, please do not make a record of these new provisions or write them at any time. You will receive this in a notification via electronically within the next work shift. Please think highly of others and remain legally determine. Thank you for being a giving faith-citizen.'

The tone ends from the intercom and my coworker, and I stare directly at it with disdain. This is the third attempt for the Global Elite to try to create a provision to the laws of the Gods. Don't know for the life of me why they would think that spirits from another realm would have a conscious and listen to some of the request men purposes to the likes of a God. After all, these spirits or God would have not intervened in our world had we not nearly destroyed it.

17

MANY PEOPLE ARE OPPOSED to joining the Council becoming a faith-citizen and propose an alternative solution to reach the level of sustainable faith for our world, to offer up to the Gods. Knowing not what Lufton knows or believes about any of this, not thinking it would be wise to ask. Something tells me that this announcement holds no need to put forward the debate.

"It is things like this that they do which made my parents change from Republicans to Democrats." Lufton seems frustrated, to say the least.

"I thought it was people like the Clintons who turned your parents into Republicans in the first place," I reply with a huge grin.

"I'm dead-serious Romas. There is no way on earth you can compare a single person to the strength and control of a God." He was in disbelief.

I understand where he is going with this, but what does it matter. "Lufton, the Elite have always known that to control the masses you must monitor their faith. I was raised in a church, and I witness people changed their faith just like night and day.

"Since the beginning of the first sophisticated civilization, the people who were above the masses immediately felt superior to the others. To put it in non-technical language, for the sake of argument, not everyone cut out to be chief. Imagine putting a complete idiot in charge of the free world. Could you now?"

I know where my co-worker is now mentally; between the establishment, and whom I consider, The Thinkers. People living in the new world still believe in free thinking and do not limit themselves to what many feel truth. "To be honest, something that is true today in the new world once was not true in the old world some forty years ago. The world or understanding of the world should be not be interpreted by the limited philosophy of the small percent who are up to the top.

The collect consciousness of the masses should not be influenced or dictated by such means as well."

Before I could get to the premise of my last thought, the lights on the ceiling turn outward and illuminate. The projector screen dims away, and we hear the doors unlock to our station. We then realize that we may have completely missed a Rapture right in front of us. My coworker storms over to his desk and at this point I don't know if it is because of the announcement or what I had just got through speaking about. Do not believe that we have missed any Raptures. Other indications transpired during our discourses. Even if glued to every single sign technology that we possess, it would be ultimately up to each individual Angel to allow us to view them in a Rapture.

Without any forewarning, the doors slide open relieving a dark haired woman from another station. She does not make any eye contact with either of us. By the looks of Lufton, he probably would creep her. "So are you guys going to sit there or do monitors not eat?" She points up at a clock we haven't seen all day. The next noise we hear is the buzz indicating that it is lunch hour, and this kind woman was giving us a head start.

The woman turns down the hallway as I slap the stupid look on my co-worker's face, I realized one of the people Lufton was staring at, coming back from the hallway during the security breach I orchestrated. *Interesting.*

We both take off our lab jackets; hang them, the shoot towards the door. After two or three steps down the hall, I quickly turn back and allow Lufton to drool after the woman. I go back inside and head straight for my lab coat. I cannot believe I almost forgot my notebook again.

Hustle down to the cafeteria to see what smells so good making the aroma fill up the vents through each station. The cafeteria is large in size, around two football fields. Lufton could be anywhere in here by now and more than likely right behind that woman. I have a brief thought as to why she came at the exact time she did. Everything happens for a reason. I just shake my head knowing that it may take an hour even to find them in the huge cafeteria, and I decide to grab some food to take with me back to our station.

Decisions, walking up to one of the ten servicing areas in the cafeteria. I know that each one of these service areas has the same meals, so I travel to the closest one to me. As I approach the counter, I notice that everyone served, and no one is waiting. I arrive at the process table and place my palm under a red light for a scan. This scan determines what types of nutrition our body is lacking, and a robot then elevates a couple of pills and a health bar. The first pill gives your liquid intake and the second tablet gives your desired flavor for the health bar. As for the bar, it dissolves in your mouth within seconds. There is no limit to how many bars or pills you can consume, and there is no need to eat for an hour. We are giving a full time so that we can stay encouraged to converspeer amongst each other. I look across the room to try to locate Lufton and this mystery woman to no avail and decided to head back to the station. This should give a head start to the next phase of my plan.

"Mr. Tate Romas." A voice sounds behind me to show Sen. Davis with his head back and eyes closed. "Where may I ask are you heading off to?"

"Sen. Davis Sir." I try not to clench my teeth. "I was actually hoping that I would run into you. I wanted to go with you up to our station so that we could go over my logs. I wouldn't want you to go out of your way at the last minute and have to stay on this island any longer than you have to."

"What in the Mother of meat for brains is your feed trap flapping about?" He replies eyes squeezed. Sen. Davis is an absolute nut case. His parents were veterans whose family were descendants in the Elite. He is a forty-five-year-old frightening man who has never served in the military, and I have to call him Sir and take orders from his shotgun shell case for brains.

"No worries, Sir." Both of my eyes closed tightly. "Was there anything I could assist you with?"

"Of course not. You couldn't pee on cue if the Queen told you to. You should never be without your wingman." He turns his back and walks away. I have no idea why that just happened. Well, everything hap… never mind. At this point, all I want to do is find Lufton, make sure everything runs on schedule and close my ears for a few consecutive minutes.

Doors open to the cafeteria as I make my out heading back to the station. I keep an eye making sure that I don't run into Sen. Davis again. I hope that I can spot my wingman. *My wingman?* The more and more I think about it; I can't seem even to leave Lufton behind now.

One left turn makes my way up to our floor. I drag my feet along the conveyor belt and let gravity carry me. A couple of steps to my left off the belt, and to turn left down our hallway. At the last second, I see a glimpse of two people down at the end of the hallway near the restrooms. The female is facing the male in my direction and looks over his shoulder at me. She then grabs his face and passionately kisses him while she stares right at me.

"You got to be kidding me?"

I drop my head backward and turn down the hallway. What guess happened? There are just some reasons why it sucks to have a photographic memory. Why me? By the drooping shoulders and Pepe Le Pew trance, I knew just how long I had until my bell leveled co-working returns to our station. If he comes back a few minutes before or after the lunch period is over, will tell me about this mystery woman. Plus, more importantly, who or what would put her up to do such a thing to an Eddie Munster looking creep head like my dear friend. The Rapture world ain't looking bad.

I reach the station and not to my surprise, I see Sen. Davis sitting at my workstation. Why he is still here, I don't know. I would have imagined that he would have gone to go get the Army since I had cleaned my log out.

Before I could think of a lie to buy myself some time, he arises from my chair and makes a b-line right to me, almost purposely.

"That is some excellent work, Romas. Keep it the good job and stay on the path."

He makes it out of the door and leaves me to stand alone with my mouth open. I sit down after storing the events that recently took place over the last 2 hours, and I put it all together. Kicking my feet up and take out my health bar. We all know that we get our sense of taste through smell. For some reason, however, I cannot taste anything. There are stale odors and pollen particle dust hovering around my workstation.

Just as I go to investigate the smell, an announcement vibrates throughout the room and along the corridor down the hall. The inanimate voice prompts as follows:

[Ding]

'Attention monitor stations sectors 2012 -2031. Monitor Lufton Magnus a5011973; please report to Council meeting room 350, immediately. I repeat, Monitor Lufton Magnus a5011973 please report to Council meeting room 350. All other monitors remain at your stations and stay determined.'

After the announcement, I completely have lost track of the smell, grinding my teeth while trying not to yell. The last thing I need is for Lufton to be in trouble at this point. Now, everything has taken a turn for the worst. Can only imagine how much of a setback losing my wingman at this stage will be. I start to overthink and worry that he may be in for some serious disciplinary actions based on his recent involvement with this woman, fired on the spot or very worst, arrested.

Whatever the case, I cannot afford to lose time. Frustrated. May not be a serious thing at all. Lufton is a crucial part of this mission. I would usually prevent something like this to happen. Still, I have complete confidence in my wingman's ability to get past severe and complexed situations. Two love birds, to be more than platonic and especially at work in the most secretive island in the world. *Ugh. What a slip-up?*

18

I KNOW THAT I MUST STAY the course and wait for Lufton to come back to assure that the rest of my friends and family can be located. This is becoming more and more intense, almost getting out of hand. Of course, this was going to be hard.

I take out a warm cloth, which was inside of a compartment where I keep my imploder. The last time I was under this much pressure was... Sweat strumming down my face during the rapture of Lon was bad enough.

Still, remembering where I am. Focus on the job at hand. I can sound off multiple programs that I know for sure I could never hack into to prevent my deception. My whole presence at this point is in jeopardy. Like it has always been. When will I be able to sleep one night without feeling like there may be a shotgun pointed at my head when I open my eyes? My eyes are open, I hope. I feel that I know more about are life, the Council, the Gods, and these Angels. I am just confused as to why now. Why in this lifetime is it happening? Why do I feel like I have to know all of these secrets? In a perfect world-, I guess there is no perfect world, so it doesn't matter what I think.

The only thing that is perfect is God. But, which God? Not the demi-Gods who control men, evil, and earth. Not these demons and Angels who our God gives orders. I am talking about the actual Creator. Who may not even be a God? Who may be and only be? The Golden ratio. Inequilaquliay, The Supreme designer, is perfect. The one who created the universe. Alternatively, the one who created life inside the firmament.

Just some things do not add up here on earth, still. No matter what you believe. Like good and bad- right or wrong. The new laws that the Gods have created are nothing like the Commandments of the Bible. Then again, in the Bible, God tells us to sacrifice, both good and bad.

In Hebrews 13:16 the Bible says;

'Do not neglect to do good and to share what you have, for such sacrifices are pleasing to God.'

For we know this is a real sacrifice meaning an act of giving up something valued for the sake of something else regarded as more important.

Then it goes on to say in Romans 12:1-2, the same book...

'I appeal to you, therefore, brothers, by the mercies of God, to present your bodies as a living sacrifice, holy and acceptable to God, which is your spiritual worship. Do not be conformed to this world, but be transformed by the renewal of your mind, that by the test you may discern what the will of God is, what is good and acceptable and perfect.'

In philosophy, teaches that the soul can go to heaven or hell, but the body stays here. In the day of the Israelites, the mind considered independent of the body. They believed that the mind was pure and the body, naturally evil. I paid some attention in school raised by a Nun.

Lastly, our world today- this new world, sums up, Psalms 106:37-41…

'They sacrificed their sons and their daughters to the demons; they poured out innocent blood, the blood of their sons and daughters, whom they sacrificed to the idols of Canaan, and the land was polluted with blood. Thus, they became unclean by their acts and played the whore in their deeds. Then the anger of the Lord was kindled against his people, and he abhorred his heritage; he gave them into the hand of the Nations so that those who hated them ruled over them.'

The Gods who rekindled our planet send demons and Angels down to us to Rapture when we kill or sacrifice others, even ourselves. And we are to believe that this is what keeps our world spinning and the Gods from destroying us. The ones who rule over us are the Global Council, and these Elitists do hate us. Almost sounds as if, everything that happens has already occurred. But, would that make everything predetermined or what is determinism?

The insurmountable lack of knowledge and truth left unavailable to the masses. In the past, the few wise desperately wanted to be on the right side of justice and not let this world draw us in psychologically. My outstretched arms relieve cramps from a prolonged folding. It feels like I am trying to yawn and catch my breath at the same time. A few hand signals directed at the coffee pot over on the center file table and my favorite brew will be ready in 30 secs. Now that I think about it, I am not sure if the coffee will wake me up or invite insomnia.

The empty chair in front of me holds a cold beat in my body. My wingman's workstation is not of interest to even a hack attempt from me. The only thing that is on my mind is if this at all is my fault. And the paper balls pile up next to Lufton's chair, aiming them at his screen in my despair. My feet flop up to my desk, my head and seat lean back to support my thoughts. My eyes close, my mind wanders. I keep speaking to myself, trying hard not to belittle, ridicule, and condemn my efforts in the mission. There is no need to put myself down, while I am letting others down.

'Can you feel that? Why are your ears ringing? It feels like the room just became warmer. Can't you tell someone is there?' I think to myself.

Before I can completely open my eyes while my head is tilting back in my chair, I see a silhouette of a person who is hovering over me. Almost losing my balance, I cut back behind me, dropping my feet off my desk to my amazement. The mystery woman is standing next to me. The woman that Lufton was involved with had managed to enter our station without my knowledge or detection. With my mouth wide open and eyes stunned, I stare with a sincere intent. The woman has pale skin and thin blonde hair. Flying dust particles surround her as if she was wearing an old Leatherman jacket locked in a closet for years, appearing familiar to me.

The woman points upward and shakes her head at me, cutting off from saying a word. I give her a slight understanding wink and manipulate the monitoring system inside of our unit shortly. A few keystrokes later, I look up to see that this woman has made it somehow to Lufton's station without me noticing. I shake it off understanding that my wingman's desk is directly in front of me, and I did not see either her movements time- when she initially came in or passing me. After another few seconds, the system alerts me that the monitors inside my unit are completely disabled and not currently able to track. The system will be unnoticeable for a short time; that whatever the reason this woman is here I will be able to find out quickly.

As I push off my desk with my hands, I roll several feet in my chair along the open workspace to get closer. The woman is dressed in a full Monitor's uniform laced with combat boots and white gloves. The only difference that I can tell is the lightness of her hair color, and her reluctance to look me directly in the eyes. The concern that I sense within her impedes my efforts in questioning and diverts my discretion to listen compassionately in hopes to converspeer.

19

THIS MYSTERY WOMAN stares at me with intent. "He will return to help you." She says. "My name is Aballah." When we do not exactly know if someone can read our direct thoughts, we become interested in what said, hoping that can repeat the statement to make it true that they can read us. I try to keep a straight face and not say a word. I have many questions to ask Aballah, but I feel as if I listen, all the information it need be present to me now.

"If you continue to believe that I can read your mind then we will have more time to discuss events taken in the worlds." She proclaims. At this point, I could not possibly know what to say or even know who she is. It is evident that she is not what she appears to be and have abilities that are more capable.

Aballah goes on, "I know you are wondering who I really am. People who are confused, everyone. Yet, some of the people who believe second and question first receive understanding at a higher level. That is why I am here, and this is where you come in. There are many things that we must discuss with the Gods, Angels, Council, and belief."

I am hanging forward off the edge of my chair with her implications. I can say that it is safe to assume Aballah may not be on any of the different levels that we have here as workers. I automatically race through my mind if she can be a hacker as I am an Angelic spirit or even an underground spy. My eyes widen, and heartbeat skips as I continue to listen.

"Through this island, lay a secret that the world has hidden for many centuries. It is the key to the mindset that controls the masses." She states. "Once the power to rule and control nations is revealed the changes necessary to stay in authority is the single best defense leaders have."

I am an expression of understanding in the making. I believe that this woman or spirit can answer any set of questions many people would kill. Being on an island meant to keep ourselves from killing one another not left to scrutiny any longer.

"You can say to yourself that Lufton and I were supposed to speak. That you and I were going to meet precisely now. How could anyone possibly be able to predict events before occurring? As even psychic ability misused as deductive reasoning, where does that leave the rest of our intuition?

"There are a few of us on this planet who do not agree with the rules of the universe in which the Gods can create and rekindle. I cannot go into too much detail with so little time. But to my understanding, you may have been selected to do more than you realize to not only help the ones you love but change the course of existence."

My understanding is completely mind boggled at the last statement Aballah made. I take a deep breath and continue to struggle to profile her. She places her feet together and stands straight up. Her shoulders move disproportionately to her body as she walks over to the display monitor. With a slide of her hand, the screen turns on, and she continues to speak to me while facing the opposite direction. "I must let you know something else about me. But first, I would like to receive your interpretation of what you believe is Predeterminism in the new world." She states.

My interpretation? I can think of several things that I am interpreting at this point, and none of them is about the new world status quo. Primarily, who is this woman and what does she know about what happened to Lufton? Secondly, how did she get in here and how can she see what I seem to be thinking? And if she can, in fact, read my thoughts, why on earth would she want to know my opinion of Predeterminism?

I might as well go ahead and face the music at this point. It is irrefutable that thinking to myself will get me anywhere else. I clench my fist tight. Interlock my hands together and direct my sight to this image. My head tilts back to the right, and I take my left hand to rub the back of my neck. I wipe off more sweat and take a deep breath.

"I must say that you seem to be more mysterious the more we meet. You call yourself, Aballah. Well, my name again is Romas." I try hard not to smirk. "I can also tell you that I don't think I'm any more special to this world then Lufton. If you do know what happened to him, I will gladly share my thoughts."

Before I can say another word a swift gust of wind passes through me, dust from her flying into my eyes. I witness Aballah clear two steps as if she floats in the air without any up and down movements. I no longer believe she is one of us. The gust of wind was strong enough to cause me to blink. I have been underground many times to know how to create illusions. This was not one of them.

Aballah steadfast the other side of the room without answering me, and as I look back to the monitor screen, I see a room with a Councilman interrogating Lufton. He sits with his back to me in a gray metal chair, surrounded by guards in military uniforms. The head person questioning Lufton is a top official- boldfaced with one arm across his desk and the other held up with a pointed finger in the air. The Councilman, uniform with ranks and ribbons, questions with direct intent.

The screen flashes off leaving me with a bit of assurance that Lufton is safe for the moment. While I sit quietly in my chair, my probe still unanswered. More than several minutes have passed, but I do not feel worried or tempered. The fact that Aballah has as much control over the monitor has me to believe we have more time to continue this dialogue. I need some answers fast.

"I thank you. As long as Lufton is okay and not in jail, I can speak with you for a while." I give a half smile. "I am sure you will share some light on what exactly you are and what the hell is going on. I read and studied my position here on the Island for 2 weeks before working my way through the gates. I still cannot tell you what Predeterminism is exactly. Ha. The Council wants us to believe it is the system implicated to save lives and obey the Gods. But why?" I do not want to seem lost, but I need more information myself.

"I mean, after all, we believe in a world of free will for so long, while the Council encourages us to stay determined. Yet, in the end, they prevent us from doing both with enforcing Predeterminism. If our actions are already predetermined, then why should we bother thinking about what to do with our futures?"

Aballah stands at the other end of the room and turns in my direction. Her hair shines brighter as dust circling her chemistry. The clouds and dust have shadowed a light color, and it seems as if this anomaly or illusion no longer needed. "For centuries your planet had a widespread belief in free will." She proclaims. "It was known by the philosophers and theologians that losing this knowledge would cause calamity throughout your civilization."

My head lifts up and turns directly to her. I had not realized what she had just said up into now. The belief of free will as a liberating civil creation. "Go on." I push my legs back and stand not surprised to taste a cold cup of coffee.

"Before I arrived, you were contemplating what right and wrong are. Your code of ethics assumes that you can freely choose between the two." She moves in closer. Her clothing follows movements unusual to normal. "If you are not to be made free to choose, then it would not be necessary to choose a path of righteousness."

"I suppose. So, where are you going with this?"

"Perhaps having free will, in the past, has helped shape the laws of the land and the rule of the world. However, the problem will automatically still persist," she continues, "The created laws of man can never trump the laws of nature or the actions of our natural genetics. In other words, our biological makeup is of the laws of what you believe to be the universe. In your history, an American physiologist Benjamin Libet had proved that there is no free will. He was able to show proof that the electrical energy that builds up in the brain causes humans to lift their arms, for example, and that this buildup occurs before the person consciously makes a decision to move."

"Yes. This is a documented reference. It also states that if we could understand any individual's brain architecture and chemistry well enough, we could, in theory, predict that person's response to any given stimulus with 100% accuracy." I reply. I walk over to refill my cup of coffee. I take a glance at the systems to see if the station detected. "So since this theory has been proven, and you have the laws of cause and effect, you can only say that we are predictable and therefore controllable."

"Yes. Eventually, you will find that if you create laws to govern the people and punish them if there break the same law, you can only morally do so if the people believe they can consciously make a decision to disobey in the first place."

Aballah has slowly shifted forms at this point and is bright as the lights. She absorbs the lights as small beams shine in the atmosphere. I understand that she is some type of spirit being and not a human. Perhaps this spirit is what I have been sensing and was following me for quite a while. With a cup full of coffee,

I turn to find this spirit completely translucent, and all I can sense is its voice. The lights inside the station reflect off dust particles allowing me to detect the entity briefly. I have many more questions now.

20

THE PLUSH RED SOFA in the far back corner of the station calls my name. Thoughts storming inside my head that I take with me, as I count the steps in the sofa's direction. Overload. I pass my workstation. I turn on the system, so I no longer have to be a prisoner of detection inside my building.

I now communicate with a spirit inside my mind and thoughts. Relieved. My face down on the sofa. I turn facing the ceiling to meditate. The spirit is no longer visible. Aballah communicates with me in my head. I have to try and not speak aloud and appear even more delusional. *I have my own Angel, now. How and b*etter yet, why?

Would much prefer a genie? Laughing while I lay on my back, I almost choke. I have no idea if there is a Supreme God or a Supreme Angel, or equal and created Gods. There is a creator; I do know that. A purpose- not by accident. Cause and an effect. Also, laws we must obey depending on where we are.

"I would like to know what happened before the wars," I ask my spirit, Angel. "I recall people who had begun to challenge the free will and the laws, claiming that they had no control over their choices and actions. Is this what started the shift of consciousness leading up to our apocalypse?"

Aballah answers, "Yes and no. It is true that people who believe less in free will are more prone to behave unethically and thus cannot blame for their actions. At the same time, society understands that seeing our actions as determined by forces we cannot control, will lessen our livelihood and sense of moral responsibilities."

I understand now that I can hear my spirit Angel speak inside my head. This Angel maybe my own manifestation or it may not. This spirit could be a collection of past souls. Guided aids. My Angel could even be from a spirit of a close relative who is no longer here with me. Dreadful to think. Inside my temporary relief turns to amusement. I toss a ball made of rubber bands in the air. It is an old hobby of mine. I visualize before the wars. Think of my Mother; how simple life used to be. Having human problems only. *Funny.*

The mass population and consciousness began to shift away from free will. A psychologist has long recognized that human behavior comes from neurophysiology. Inevitably, we are products of nature and are subject to the laws of cause and effect. Thus so, many began to believe in determinism. That our brains connected to nature, are the source of our actions. That even if we were to repeat the same action 100 times given free will of choice, we ultimately would produce the same effects.

Don't know if I am completely buying into this logic. But, the shift to determinism happened. Evil determined to create. The one world Globalization of control. Wars and overthrown Governments. Population control with GMO's, diseases, vaccinations, chemical warfare, and Global warming to name a few.

However, I am perplexed at how nature could allow this determinism to be. "If everything is determined, and everything happens for a reason, does nature want to destroy us?" I question Aballah. I get no response after a few moments pass. I realized that my Angels might have a time limit. On the other hand, could it be something else? *Was this another crazy dream?*

My knees hit the floor as I roll over to my right side down to the payment. A dim flash and a soft buzz turn on the large monitor. To my surprise, I see the room, which Lufton is in, pop back up on the screen. In his hands, he holds an alertus. It appears that he and the device explaining his earlier logs to the Councilmen questioning him. He is brilliant enough to patch a feed over to me as well. "Thanks, buddy."

The scene is familiar. Two Guards on both ends. A second yet older Councilman at the table now, opposite of Lufton. The Councilman uniform of the same as the first. His hair shows experience and face authority. Good cop- bad cop, perhaps. Lufton sounds quite amused by the line of questions at this point. He figured he could let me in on his joy. I am glad that he did.

The Councilman's name is Cpt. Willis. I quickly patch his bio on my workstation's screen. He is an American war hero. At least that is what it says here. It is frequent or severe to be whom you are not around here. Cpt. Willis demeanor is relaxed and calm. There is almost a settled happiness in comparison to the first Councilman. I raise my hand directly upward giving the signal to lock the entrance automatically.

Speakers turned up and system secured, I listen in to Lufton's feed. "We can go over my logs today, but I have to tell you that I only schedule a visit for next week. He is a faith citizen who fears he will be Raptured for having gastroparesis." My wingman can barely keep his straight face.

The first Councilman begins to stand up and lean towards Lufton. Cpt. Willis grabs his colleague's arm squeezing him down. "Councilman, please." He proceeds. "You may be dismissed. Thanks for your initial interviewing expertise, and have your submitted report to me by 18:30, please."

"Understood, Sir." The Councilman and the two guards leave out of the room. Cpt. Willis' hand signals to lock the door automatically. Several clicks. The steel walls filter voices on the other side. I only see the back of Lufton fathead, and I can tell that he is smiling ear to ear. He takes a collectible pencil out of the Captain's coffee mug. Lufton carelessly flips the rare pencil in the air, dropping it several times.

What an idiot?

"Do you know why you are here, Sir?" He stares him down. "If you do then please tell me. It is people like you who make people like me miss the Armageddon days."

"I do apologize Captain, but I found a lovely lady to converspeer with, and now I am here."

"Is that why you are here, shit stain?" He catches the pen in midair. "I would much rather you be here staining these walls."

Lufton suddenly becomes stiff. "Well, in that case maybe I do know why I am here, Sir. I did want to know- if you could shed a little light that could bounce off these flat walls for me." My fingers interlocked behind my head. Tilt on my chair. I am almost tempted to order some retro popcorn. Lufton is a complete fool. He may just get the right type of information, however.

"You know what, I appreciate you. These walls were shined before you got here." He jokes. "Fair enough, what is it that you need to know?"

"What do you call a faith citizen who doesn't understand what The Great Truth is, Sir?"

"What is this, happy hour?" He asks. "I don't know. Enlighten me. What do you call someone who doesn't know, 'The Great Truth?'?"

"You're shining wall servant, Sir."

Cpt. Willis's face turns beet red. "Hahaha. You are as dumb as your file says you are, Magnus!" I never saw a man choke as hard as now. I can only imagine the pure wide-eyed expression on Lufton's face.

Stunned. His foolishness may have paid off. Seems as if he has read the Captain's soft spot for Dummies manual. *Hilarious.*

Several minutes spent with the Captain gasping for air, drooling, and drying his tears. Lufton through up a few funny hand signals for me to see. The worst was that one of the hand signals flickered the lights to catch the Captain's attention, as I reached towards the screen virtually to choke Lufton.

"You are about as bright as a night light," says the Captain, "but I doubt you know what that was. So let me help aluminate the perspective on human civilization."

21

FEW MINUTES OF SILENCE passes in the room of the two men from a dark transpired commentary. The right side of the Captain's desk displays a monitor screen embedded under the glass top. A binary beat of theta waves plays across the speakers omitted from a pearl case sound system in the four upper corners. Lufton and I both cannot bare the humming work cooler breakroom of a tone. However, Captain Willis seems to take ease.

After reading a few full digital emails, the Captain addresses my sidekick. "You know, when I first decided to get into the type of work that I do, it wasn't because I wanted to make a difference in the world. Not at all. It was out of fear. Fear. I said to myself, 'War is emanated, as long as we are in the game, this rat race.' We do not have a choice in whether or not we are involved.

"I wasn't a young man afraid of protecting his family against the evils of the world. It was just me, alone. I have no family at all. That was not the problem. I was one of those evil men, and I did not want to continue to be. My eyes were opened the day I understood that the choices I had to make were already done for me."

"You are talking about compatibilism- that free will is compatible with determinism? As long as our mind is one cause in the causal chain that we can be responsible for our actions, which is reasonable. But you think every reason, including our decisions, are pre-determined?" Lufton states. "That is the definition, correct?" He types The Great truth into his alertus as well.

"The Great truth motto reads: 'We are one in all and all in one. There are no men but only the great We, One, indivisible and forever.'"

"You will peel off your fingertips before you find any answers on that prowling contraption, solider." The Captain turns his head. "Civilness created in the beginning- a bunch of compatibilist chickens running around this planet, indivisible and under God. Without a supreme God, there is no accountability. So ultimately, left with more than one set of laws, the laws of nature, the laws of man, and the law of God. Stay with me. There are reasons that some explanations are untold.

"Let me ask you this question? How would you know about my party I will be having on my 70th birthday, coming up?" Ask the Captain.

"You would have to invite me somehow, Captain."

"Now tell me, why the hell would it be I urge you to something like that?"

"I assume you feel that I would like to go, or that I should be a part of your celebration. Maybe, you wanted me to meet your friends and family."

"I would invite you to be with my family is right. I don't have any friends. Friends are only real enemies." The Captain states.

"With all due respect, Sir- what does this have to do with anything?" Lufton spats.

I am ahead of Lufton on what the Captain is eluding. I read that some of the top leaders that are in the Council had been descendants of the deepest secret organizations the world has ever known. Even to this day, some of the senior leaders in these organizations and sects are not aware of all the secrets. In other words, this is no quick search or app for this matter.

"Well, let's just say that you are in luck today. When the Predeterminism protocol is in full implication, every employee in this building will know what the real meaning of the Truth. So, I would be more than resourceful to tell you some secrets now." He states. "Don't worry; we can skip over the rituals, human sacrifices, bone and skull crushing, and mutilation for now." Sgt. Willis gives out an enormous laugh, stands to his feet, and bends over touching both kneecaps. His humor does not agree with Lufton.

The decorative hero mentors around his steel desk with the high-tech digital glass top. He makes a pass behind Lufton casually grazing his hand across my excited colleague's back. Lufton's feet come together as he begins to push up on the chair only to feel the weight of the Captain's hand reseat him. I would be on my second bowl of popcorn by now. Captain Willis tall stature and build intimidates many, and his intellect is renowned to trump most converspiring before it begins. He is a man who gets his point across.

"I didn't make it this far to become compatible, Mr. Magnus." He scowls. "The honest truth is that without fear of a Superior Being or leader, we humans would eventually understand that we are not accountable for what happens with our own individual actions. Once made aware that we are our conscious and that, we have an awareness of so-called being or self; we have eaten from the forbidden tree. Without any knowledge of what we are, doing is inherently right or wrong, to never held accountable. Consciousness has now become an entity inside our being, and ever since metaphysics and spirituality shifts, awareness has become a perception instead of creation.

"Atheism, Satanism, Christianity, religion, doctrines, Gods, Idols, Deities, and so on; are all creations. Created to shift consciousness from the one true God and we have attempted to please the God that rules over each of these. Whichever God is in control." Captain Willis paces around the floor. His durable military boots snatch the fibers from the Global council's carpet seal. He takes a small towel with him returning to his seat as he dabs his forehead. Lufton is left stunned with his mouth half opened.

What did he mean by whichever God is in control?

I can sense these are the same thoughts running through Lufton head as he sits with a blank expression. Up into the last point, the Captain had made, I was well aware of. Although, most of the briefing is foreign to my colleague he is now aware of more than any other employee in the compound is. With that being the case, he will more than likely end up in the tank for the remaining shift to receive some reprogramming. I have concluded that Lufton should remain safe and has managed to gather the information I needed him to have, all from an unlikely source.

I have more questions remaining unanswered as the live feed terminates from the Captain's office by my wingman. I presume that I have at least fifteen minutes left to continue hacking into Captain Willis's personal files before Sen. Davis stumbles into the station from the security breach. I am hoping to find out more about the Captain before I continue with my mission. He mentioned the Gods that are in control. *Wishing that Lufton had asked about the Angels.*

Six different times the lights flickered in my station as I go through the files. The complex on the island is massive in size and powered by solar generated energy, backup generators as large communities with the wind and water propulsions systems. In other words, I could plug in a toaster the size of the Sydney Opera House with no problem. The lights seem out of the ordinary, however. *Nothing is out of the ordinary.*

I gather my alertus and close out the files on my workstation. Been inside of this room for too much time. Approximately 19:08. Time is not on my side because we have transported to the Raptures in a few short hours. Cannot connect with Aballah, almost of if the entire encounter was a dream. I also must use a Vactrain to reach the other side of the island to reprogram transports for the leader Cain. All of this while wearing a big smile to avoid suspicion. *Yeah, right.*

Everything put away and locked up inside of the station as I make my way down the corridors. It is usual for me to be out and about the island. The Council put into regulations that all employees can tour the entire complex at least once a year. The next thing you know, it replaced our yearly vacations, and so, I have my reasons to be anywhere; that is not restricted at least.

I hope I don't look too much like a Starship Trooper with this tan and green satchel.

The corridor lights up with amber color detecting my mood and temperament. Being a Monitor and knowing the ends and outs has to help me make it this far. I take out my virtual display pad to calculate the time I will reach the other side of the compound, where they hold the individual capsules. We Monitors like to joke and call it the Hippodrome Palace Island, where you come to lay rolled like a pig in a blanket of sweet dreams. To my calculations, minus personal distractions, I should make it there under two hours.

22

MY UNDERTONE MANTRA calms me down the monitor's facility. "Har Hare-Haree Wahe Guru. Har Hare-Haree Wahe Guru. Har Hare-Haree Wahe Guru." Across my neck is an all-access card that transmits a hologram image code, connecting to unlock the doors with a few feet's distance. I keep my breaths and pace to control my surroundings as I continue on to the vactrains.

Technology has slowly shifted back to science engineering, teleportation engineering, anti-gravity, neurosciences, and the recent comeback transhumanism. The best part of the day for me is the replacement of elevators with air chambers. The Council was even thoughtful enough to add aromatherapy.

My hologram image code tags to the silver door opening the air chamber to the vactrains. It's, of course, wise to secure any loose items while on board. One-step inside the bottomless elongated single manned tube controls the airflow, preventing me from falling to my death. The pulsating jets maneuver me tighten body through the human chimneys at sporadic speeds. The best part is the descent to the floor I am requesting. A few seconds hovering in the chamber a couple feet off the ground until the air pressure dissipates me to the floor. I step outside the tube now.

I am ahead of schedule on my way to the vactrains, so there is no need to ride on the wall tram. I think the trams are a bit silly- sitting chairs placed next to each other attached to the wall traveling 15 miles per hour is a bit lazy. I guess if you are in a rush you would have to take a ride. The distance to get to some trains can take up to 40 minutes each walking. Nonetheless, I feel as if I am in several airports traveling an infinite distance- all to find my gate.

I reach a tunnel, which leads me several hundred feet from my vactrain. Pulling around my body, checking inside my satchel for all my belongings. I see guards hauling citizens to an incarceration vactrain heading for the same transport station. Mostly all of the citizens are docile and sedated except one man. The faith-citizen is asking many questions, and I can assume that he may even be a volunteer to the Raptures. Few people come willingly to the Island knowing that the Predeterminism technology will save them from the Angels, and yet some still come due to impatient helplessness.

"I never got a full answer from you, Sir." The man addresses a guard. "Can you please tell me which module I will be in, and how long of a duration will I be down?" The guard ignores the man pleas for information and viciously pushes him forward causing the electromagnetic straps across his body suit to send out a sharp volt. Another curious inquiry and the citizen will be heading to the organ transplant station. The Council security guard forces are notorious for accidentally allowing persons to terminate.

"Hey buddy, relax and let these men do their job," I advise the person.

"What's it to you?"

"Do you see the flickering lights in this super compound, Sir?" I harp. "Well, it is known as an anomaly. That means that it does not happen, and it is out of place. Something like the demons, you are trying to avoid. That is why you are here, correct?"

The guard places his hand over his baton ready to grip. "Just keep moving."

"He is fine, Sir," I claim. "In fact, I will ride in the incarceration train with you both. My name is Romas Tate; Security Monitor A-5001462." The guard takes a snarl look at me up and down; then he releases the citizen to me as we all enter the train. I give the man a pat on the back and help him into the supersonic train, strapping him in. The other prisoners, who are at least attentive, stare with disparity.

"Don't know what to say," the man claims, "I thought this guy was going to kill me for asking so many questions." The security guards skate along the lines of breaking the God laws by allowing a citizen to die while traveling the transport. Their morals are just above mind-stalks in the underground, in a sense, who knows how to manipulate someone to think negative thoughts, in efforts to commit the citizen to suicide. However, at the Council Island, we can detect any evil spirits within an hour before their manifestation inside the compound, thus making the cold-hearted guards somewhat safe. Some say that the demon would have to be Luke Skywalker to breach the Island undetected. *Supernatural detection.* I guess the old televisions shows were on to some truths decades ago.

"No need to apologize," I say, "people who ask for questions often end up solving problems for us all. So what do they call you?"

"My name is Thomas."

"Well, it is pleased to meet you. Just relax. It will be a long ride." The man seems to be a volunteer to the Island indeed. He is troubled, to say the least, scarred and fragile. I can see some relief on his face from my kind intervention. To him in a way, drawn. It pays to stay on your toes. By boarding the train along with these prisoners, I can cut off almost a half hour arriving at the transport station ahead of schedule. All of the other trains lead to a separate area- a touring facility that then travels over to the station where this faith-citizen induce a coma and sent into the Rapture realms.

The most interesting part of the experience is that the employees of the Island can view the whole processing protocol. An individual human capsule will Tram across an enclosed barricaded viewing room. People line up on the other side of reinforced glass- as if this were a wild animal exhibit in a zoo. The capsule comes across and halts in the center of the room. Within minutes, the cylinder holding the citizen filled with gasses instantly passing them into the coma. Lastly, neurological electromagnetic waves fill into the victim and enclosure, sending them into a parallel state- another mental realm, indefinitely. *What am I doing?*

I have to be aware of the citizens I am on the vactrain with. Some of these people onboard may be from the underground. I cannot risk having thoughts of my plans run through my head while a telepath may subconsciously be reading me. Would not make much of a difference at this point. Everyone here on the ride will end up Raptured within a few days going through the processing phases; all except the guards. My plan is to create my own Rapture and meet up with Cain on the other side. I just hope the program I ran sends Cain into the precise realm of Rapture 6 and myself as well- not to end up inside the lower three, or even worst, Zell. The last of the passengers are strap tightly and the door shut.

A few guards and the citizens and I speed through the mountain, finally reaching our destination. Once we arrive at the processing center of the compound, I make my way into the chambers. A large station full of amber lights, with metal rails and catwalks, run miles long. The sounds of vents and pressure systems echo like caves in the distance. The temperature inside the chamber is under 30 degrees Fahrenheit. Each step that I take to reach my rapture capsule precedes deep breaths that blowout in the air. I finally reach the area where I suspect Cane will be transported from. To my calculations, we should be near each other, and possibly be in the same wave. My brow begins to sweat.

"Okay. Now I can start the protocol and sequence our raptures." I use the device I brought along with me and program the hack directly to the chip attached to the hatch of my capsule. The capsule extends out of the section inside of the large incubator-holding tank. "This is it." I found a place to hide my belongings, and I hurry back to get inside of the pod.

The main concerns that I will leave with will be if Cane rapture goes as scheduled. This way I will not have to worry about the program detecting me. It may take another day before the Council sends his group to the chambers due to the length of processing the intakes. The other concerns are what I will find once I get on the other side. I trust Cane knows more than I do. After all, he has been studying the raptures for a decade, and I know he would not deceive me. It does not matter anymore. I cannot go back.

The people I am heading to Rapture 6 to find are my focus. Of course, I know that it will not be that easy to get them standing at the front gates, waiting for me. There are rules in the different realms. The only way to find my friends and any information about my Mother is to go to the Rapture. From there I will await Cane. Until then, I can question as many Rotters I see, to know if any of them have seen Lon.

The air pressure builds in the metal framed capsule, and the hatch contracts down to lock me inside. Seconds after, the gasses begin to fill the inside of the pod as it retracts into the incubator; the technology of the entire process in superior and advanced. This process will take several minutes to complete. My eyes are dull and weak. The air is thin now. I feel the capsule propel down a chute onto a railing inside the massive docking station. My mind slowly wanders with questions that float in my head. I have programmed the rapture to transport me for several weeks. *I don't want to see anything close to an Angel.*

Well aware of what I am heading to, I know the rapture world is entirely different from the new world.

Not to worry about the Rotters and mind-stalks. Probably will know most of those heathens anyway. Only the horrible conditions of the rapture world concern me and of course demons. I am not that worried about it. I just need to blend in and be there when Cane arrivals. The first of the magnetic neural pulses startle me. *I can handle the pain.* This is a walk in the park, compared to the other routed citizens take. I know that all of my molecules will stay here inside of the capsules, all in one piece. I could not imagine the physical torcher the demon put on the people who ascend through the heavens. The virtual pain is all mine. I begin to take deep breaths. Soon I will be unconscious. Soon I will be in the Rapture World.

The pain feels like a static jolt of energy inside of my head. My mouth of dry and lips are peeling off. *Ugh!* I cannot see anything. I feel a glob of spit or something inside of my eyes. Not even able to focus. My hand is on a tree I believe, and it seems as if the dirt is falling off it clogging up my nose. As I attempt to pull myself up the limb snaps, and I roll hard. I still cannot open my eyes, but I feel giant bugs covering my body. As I swipe the insects off, I fall back, rolling down a rocky embankment causing me to bump my head impacts the bottom. I don't know what moist drips on my face as I finally come to. I just hope it is not blood. I take the next 20 minutes to gather myself, realizing where I am. I am here.

I find a shiny rock and scrap 'Day 1' on a boulder.

What is Science Prediction?

We are fortunate to live in a world of vast imaginations. Here in this world lives an infinite source of creative power. We can substantially envision our own destinies to manifest a creative work of artistry within vibrational, spiritual and emotional thoughts. We naturally are truly creative people, singers, poets, musicians, artists and so on. When such artists empower the compilation of great ideas over time, we come to piece together our stories, which we are here on earth to demonstratively conclude and experience through one other. In today's world, these written tales can be composed of standard categories we can find in every new bookstore.

Readers and authors alike fall into different classes or genres of literature based on categories and classification of the book. We tend to fall into these groups religiously. Until now, the Author's writing dream come true in an original uncategorized philosophical style of composition, which is rightfully entitled as, 'Science Prediction.'

What is Science Prediction? The answer to this question is opening and uncomplicated. Science Prediction is composing literature based on the past, and present generational events that predict a future outcome determined through theorized scientific elements. When producing Science Prediction fiction, the author attempts to capture their storylines by infusing them into our past and present reality, while utilizing scientific theory to implement the author's plot to create a future relative state of conscious life.

Science Prediction, correspondingly formulated by documenting the past and present historical events within throughout the storylines to maintain the reader's conscious reality. By doing so, this allows the user to develop the correlation between the events until the author's future scientific outcome transpires beyond the plot. This also keeps the reader from equating Science Prediction as fiction or other forms of known written literature genres.

The most important aspects of Science Prediction are a philosophical theory, theodicy, and mindfulness. The philosophical theory of Eternalism is the scientific basis of Science Prediction. Eternalism is the view that time resembles space and thus past and future events are in some sense coexistent. With this explanation, the author must explain each of its laws Science governs to make a real storyline and theory. When an artist creates Science Prediction literature, he or she commits to a theorized summary of the life and universal existence based on scientific principalities towards developing plots of unforeseen future events.

In essence, Science Prediction is a breakthrough gateway to an author's ability to create a work of theoretical artistry literature, maintaining the reader's level of conscious reality beyond fairytale or folklore, inclusive with an elaborate and purposeful scientific foretelling. In other words, Science Prediction has more intellectual offerings than Science Fiction, Science non-fiction, fiction, time travel and alternative history, etc., or any other spiritual new age literature, that only allows the audience a modern and post-modern fictitious dictation.

About the Author

Charles is an author and motivating spiritual teacher specializing in dynamic business creation and concepts. Charles's anticipated publication, Rapture World VI, set to release later in August 2016. This will be his first book of the series, 'Predeterminism.' The novel is a fictional post-apocalyptic portrayal of the world destroyed and rekindled by the new laws of the Gods. Rapture World VI is an amazing part of the sequels in the epic six-part series.

Charles is also a dedicated thinking creator. He plans to release his second book of this series this year and will begin to write his new form of fiction for authors and writers to enjoy, Science Prediction fiction. This book is a small sample of what the new kind of writing details as well as an introduction to a book on how to compose your own Science Prediction novel. Thanks for purchasing the book and stay tuned for the remaining series of Predeterminism.

For more information, contact:

charlesfendersonjr@gmail.com

http://www.facebook.com/charlesfendersonjr

http://www.zirecompany.com

Printed in Great Britain
by Amazon

74753257R00124